spying on strange men

Carole Morin was born in the east end of Glasgow. At 16 she was a Junior Diplomat to the United States where she tested the boundaries of diplomatic immunity.

She has been writer-in-residence at Wormwood Scrubs prison and Literary Fellow at the University of East Anglia.

She has beaten Stanley Kubrick in a dessert-eating contest, drunk mojitos with Fidel Castro, and been mistaken for Graham Greene's Eurasian daughter in Hanoi.

She lives in Soho.

spying on
strange men

carole morin

Dragon Ink
London

First published in the UK 2012 by Dragon Ink Ltd,
London W1F 7SJ.

orders@dragoninkbooks.co.uk

A CIP catalogue record for this book is available from the
British Library.

ISBN 978-0-9572089-0-2

Typeset by Dink London

Printed in the UK by
Imprint Digital, Devon EX5 5HY.

For

华森

Acknowledgements

Thanks to:
Millie Smith, Harry Evans,
Stanley Kubrick, Frank Budgen,
Sarah Lowe, Vivien Lash,
evil twins Silver and M-Tang
and especially to Don Watson,
who makes everything possible.

'I am really only myself when I'm somebody else.'
Zelda Fitzgerald

It was easy, once I'd decided to kill him.

Having something to focus on gives shape to your days. You don't need to worry about anything else.

Shopping in Shanghai, drinking mojitos in Havana, eating custard apples in Hanoi, trying on jewellery in Jaipur, walking about Damascus maybe, thinking of you.

Or reading every book on poison in the London Library.

Writing is prophesy.

Don't write anything unless you want it to come true. Don't say it out loud even in the dark. Because I can't afford to make a mistake. One slip and you're dead.

Why am I whispering?

The words have been written in my diary.

Writing things down is dangerous. Ink can't be erased without leaving a mess behind. Now he has to die. It's just a question of how and when.

Like a detective story with a killer and a victim but no plot. God isn't in the details, He's in the structure.

None of this shows on the surface yet. My face is the same even when I say the words out loud three times with

the full moon staring me out.
     Kill him kill him kill him.

It's best that way.
     Best for me, anyway.

He doesn't suspect.
     I don't think he suspects. You can never be sure what someone else is thinking. After all, he trusts me and I'm planning his murder.
     I assumed he'd carry on playing the same part, the adoring husband who travels for work but always comes home, the role he's been acting to perfection for years.
     That was my first mistake.

The Beginning

'If I bore you it will be with a knife.'
Louise Brooks

We slept with the windows open, keeping the grilles locked, the scent of jasmine wafting in.

We live on the ground floor of a mansion block. Our apartment is like a little house, white and seductive; London audible on the other side of the wall.

We're not wealthy though people imagine we are because we almost live in Mayfair. My husband has an expense account. I dabble in creative projects. My latest addiction is art.

We're the kind of couple people envy. We get invited to glamorous parties, but don't always go.

There I am, sleeping on white satin sheets, dreaming I'm a character in *The Blue Dahlia*.

I dream in black and white the colour of my hair and skin. The ambiguous edges smudging to silver when I paint my eyelids, maybe.

When I wake up, the first thing I see is his face, shining with happiness in our wedding picture. But this morning, propped up against the photograph on my glass dressing-table, is a large cream envelope. There's no name written on it, but I know it's for me.

I sniffed it before opening, I don't know why. The paper had a sweet scent, or maybe that's the glue used to seal it?

Inside were photographs of a girl I've never seen before. She looks Russian or Polish. A coarse Slav who'll be fat and faded before her 19th birthday. Some people feel obligated to live down to their caricature.

Enter the maid, giving a creaking curtsey somewhere between mockery and entertainment.

'Sorry Miss, I didn't know you was up.' James insists that Miss is a compliment. I don't look old enough to be Madam.

'Where did this come from?' I waved the envelope but her eyes went straight to the picture, face down on my dressing-table.

'Out of a camera, Miss.'

'Who *delivered* it?'

'The front desk sent it round first thing with a big bunch of them lilies you like and I put that there while you was asleep in case it's important, Miss.'

Has she looked in the envelope? Is she gloating? Or is her face just set in its usual sour pout?

I dressed without showering, something that gives me the creeps, and ran to reception hoping to catch the night porter before he finished his shift.

But Elvis the Porter wasn't on duty last night when the envelope was delivered.

'Good things come in the night, Miss. Like Santa Claus.' He lowered the zip on his jumpsuit, flashing a bit of chest to his nervous audience.

'Normally Elvis would have been here, on account of me being the night porter. But I've been working nights on my own account, so Elvis is here during the day.'

He tapped his nose, leaning in close so that I could smell his breakfast. Shite on toast, also known as Marmite.

'Elvis has an idea, Miss.'

We huddled together in the security room, checking the building's CCTV.

There I am, walking down the garden path in my ironic white skinny jeans. There's my husband, getting out of a taxi, back from his travels. There you are, in reception talking to Elvis.

At first glance I thought you were James. I had to rewind, look again, catch you emerging from your vintage red Jaguar. You could be his younger brother. Except he doesn't have a brother.

What are you up to? Delivering flowers, that old excuse. You have come to see where I live, to gloat because you own a big house with a swimming pool and I live in a flat with a communal garden.

The view shifts from reception. I appear again on the garden path, looking fat from this angle. Those white skinnies are going on the bonfire.

'Around and around it goes, Miss,' Elvis said. 'Welcome to Heartbreak Hotel.'

The camera spies on the car park, watching my creepy neighbour sleep in his car. When it comes back to reception, the large cream envelope is on the desk.

'Like Elvis said, Miss, it appeared in the night.'

'Like Santa Claus.'

'It's not Christmas for yonks yet, Miss, but Elvis can offer you a ginger snap.'

Is there any point in me talking to the other porter, Miguel, who's always asleep with a half-eaten Mars Bar in his mouth?

'Elvis has plans to become a Dick, Miss.'

And there was me and the rest of the world thinking he was one already.

I sat on my white bed allowing my mind to go blank so that the answer would come.

I could destroy the picture. Pretend I haven't seen it?

Why?

What does it mean?

You know what it means.

My life is a mess and I don't know how to fix it. There's a mysterious solution I can't quite grasp. Maybe it's a question of tenses?

The characters are not the problem it's the sequence. Without her there couldn't be you?

I know what I have to do.

His computer is in his dressing-room behind his bathroom.

Why does he keep it in there? Why does he lock up his clothes?

Feeling ridiculous, like I was acting the part of someone older and uglier than me, I stole the maid's key and searched his underwear drawer for clues. His spare passport, one of his phones.

The evidence must be here. Times, dates, credit card bills. Encrypted in technology. If only I knew the password.

I know the fucking password.

It's my name, unless he's changed it to her name.

The solution and the mess are the same thing. Left and right change sides when you turn around but east and west are always in the same place. I can see better with my sunglasses on.

There I go again! Imagining sight and blindness, like intimacy and separation, are opposite ends of the spectrum. Thinking I can clear things up with a shift of perspective, a change of scene, a new boyfriend.

Why would I even imagine I can control the future when I definitely didn't control the past?

When I had finished snooping I was at a loose end so I ran a bath.

He's been careful. No names. A good spy. X in Moscow. Y in London. No sign of Z yet. Unless that's her in the photograph?

No telephone numbers. I could steal his phone and call every number until a slut answers. But I draw the line at making myself ridiculous.

As Aeschylus must have said already, without betrayal there's no drama.

Knowledge is power. Without information, I can't get revenge. If I had an address or even a name for, let's call her Z, I could send a dead chicken in the mail.

But I don't. So I checked that the maid had gone, peeled off my clothes, and stepped into my bath just in time.

Our wedding picture caught my eye. There's one in every room, spying on me.

The clarity of his complexion makes him look innocent. In movies, the villain is pockmarked. So in real life good skin has come to mean good faith. Where is he now, that boy I married? Where am I?

Angry in my pink marble bathtub plotting a murder. The bath full of rose petals picked on a moonlit night. He spat on my heart with his betrayal.

Betrayal is a cliché.

Does his romance convert me into a victim? Has he won again, beat me to it, devised his escape route? Bought her *presents*? Those miscellaneous expenses from shops I haven't heard of can't all be surprises for me.

Why would the stinky little slut send me a picture she doesn't even look that good in? How the fuck does she even know where we live? James is so secretive he has secrets even from himself.

Maybe the ho-bag didn't intend the picture for me? It's a present for him. Something to remember her by? A warning? But if the envelope was for him, it would have his name on it.

When I come out of the bath, he's home.

His heart has no home. He gets nervous when love circles him. Panics when happiness closes in. Should I laugh out loud or bite him?

'Hello Baby,' he says, like nothing's changed. He looks innocent. We are still the perfect couple. 'We're going to the Russian Riviera.'

The Black Sea

Once I'd decided to murder him, he was allowed to touch me again.

At the Russian Riviera, people made the usual jokes about 21st century spies, how the job has changed - more Austin Powers than James Bond. No one explained what the conference was about, and I wasn't interested anyway.

On the first day I sat under an umbrella by the Black Sea, one foot in the water. Is he thinking about Slut Z, wondering if he'll manage to avoid her? Did he meet her last time he was here?

Is she a spy? Most men meet their bitch at work. He was working when he met me. Had they exchanged adolescent emails before fixing a date to fuck or 'make love' as whores like her creepily call it? Is she here now, watching me with my toes in the water?

I scanned the beach for the ho-bag in the photograph. There are lots of girls with skinny limbs and a titanic ass. She looks like a Pisces: wet and sneaky in the digital image she hand-delivered.

Does she have pictures of him looking younger than his age?

In a movie I'd have to catch them in the act. A young bum heaving on top of him. There are no compromises in backsides these days. They are either gigantic or invisible.

In an art installation this could be dealt with in stills arranged beside a used condom, her soiled (so last century) thong, the lip-stained glass she drank from after the act.

Anyway she looks the type to have a soiled thong stuck in the crack between her bloated bum cheeks. And the lipstick would have to be orange like her out-of-date hair.

Once I'd decided to escape once and for all, seduction was like a killer's kiss.

On the second morning, windows open allowing the scent of pine trees to infiltrate the room, I initiated it by rubbing against him, lying on my side, him behind. At first he thought it was a mistake, I must be asleep. But I persisted then turned myself over and had him that way.

After dressing, he came back to kiss me goodbye. He stood at the edge of the bed watching me sleep, nervous but pleased, unaware of my plan.

It's easier to drift along doing nothing.

Giving up your ideals, as Great-aunt Tatiana said

when she was alive, is the road to heartache. And later or sooner, you get the life you desire. The life we dreamed that summer in Trieste when there were no strawberries and I insisted on walking to Greece in the wrong shoes.

My best friend wanted to come with me but she was scared.

'It's too far,' Tasha said.

'Come on!' I shouted. I've always wanted to escape. It's still my favourite daydream.

'I'm scared,' she said. I was still close enough to see her tears.

'It will be all right,' I smiled, grinning maniacally up at the stars.

I kept on walking. She went back. I escaped. And I went on and on escaping until I met James.

Of course I want to change my mind, allow myself to love him again.

I recognise the smell of his skin, I admire his eyelashes when he's sleeping. If I close my eyes, I can see our heads close together on the silk pillow.

But it's too late. I am bored with betrayal. I intend to deny myself nothing. Let the husband be careful.

Murder is an ending. A declaration of war is a beginning. Anything can happen!

If I hadn't seen the picture, the option of pretending would still be there.

There is no evidence that she exists except that photograph. The coarsening of her nose from too many toxins already visible to the camera. A shadow of her future, the double chin she will soon have, revealed by the flash. I couldn't resist slashing her a new smile.

I couldn't destroy the photograph, or leave it sitting on the table. So I hid it somewhere he might find it. And now I have to act casual, go about my business like nothing's up, so that he suspects nothing.

Just carry on as normal spying on strange men.

Creepy Neighbour

My installation has been arrested.

The fraud squad came at dawn and took him away.

'He has documents hidden in the vault,' Elvis told me, full of his own importance.

Elvis had seen the action live. I was watching it on CCTV. Thanks to me, there's a camera pointed at my creepy neighbour's door.

He comes out at 8.32 carrying a briefcase, wearing his three-piece suit, the button on the waistcoat straining over his belly. At 8.49, Creepy Neighbour lets himself back in. He is out and in all day, usually carrying a large black bin bag stuffed full of...?

No one has seen his wife in the flesh for weeks. The joke in the building is that she's in the bin bags. But there she is, on camera, leaving for work. She's alive. She just isn't his wife.

During the day, I spot Creepy Neighbour around the neighbourhood. He's wearing enormous purple gloves, whatever the weather, using a payphone in our street, his phone sticking out of his pocket.

Last week, I stood in the queue behind him, my own phone ringing in my bag. I switched it off. Creepy Neighbour put on a pair of Jackie O sunglasses.

Maybe they are his mother's; maybe he bought them in Poland Street in the Asian shop with the almost-cool accessories?

After he had used the payphone and wiped the handset, I went in and pressed the code an engineer at BT taught me for last number redial. A woman answered.

She shouted, 'Cunt! Don't call me again.' A girlfriend?

Elvis said no. Lowering his loud voice to a loud whisper, he told me, 'Number Four terrorises witnesses for a lawyer.'

Number Four. It makes him sound like an exotic crap. The thing that comes after a Number One (urine), a Number Two (excrement), a Number Three (diarrhoea).

Number Four, Creepy Neighbour, was my live show. I was working up to inviting him to appear at the gallery, standing inside a white circle, wearing the purple gloves.

I paid Elvis to check the building's security system for sightings of Creepy, then give the tapes to me instead of allowing them to go round and round; erasing themselves.

I bought a pair of night sights so that I could look in his bedroom window and see if he is having creepy sex with Mrs Creepy, the woman who isn't his wife. Creepy's windows, like mine, are conveniently located on the ground floor of our mansion block, overlooking the communal garden.

This voyeurism is an ironic role reversal. Voyeur (me) becomes Creepy Neighbour by indulging in this peeping tom activity.

I wore big black leather gloves the first night, but had to take them off halfway through the spy session because they were making me giggle. I made a mental note. Buy purple gloves. Purple is the theme of this show.

There was no sexual activity in their bedroom, but I did see Creepy Neighbour naked.

He has a deep vertical crease in his stomach, which makes it look like a bum. Kneeling outside his window, peering through the crack in the curtains with my night sights on, his head cut out of the shot, I couldn't tell if I was looking at him from the back or the front. He has a bum on both sides.

In my black leather notebook, I wrote in wet black ink: *He doesn't appear to have a penis.* This puzzled me the next day. The ink had smudged while drying, and it looked like: *He doesn't appear to have a pen.*

There was a curious moment when I thought there were two of him. A double take through the crack in the curtains confirmed this impression, and I took a few quick shots with my James Bond spy camera - bought from a shop for big grown up spies in South Audley Street, a few doors down from where Audrey Hepburn lived when she was a chorus girl in London.

I ran home to wake my husband.

'Creepy Neighbour has a twin!' I shrieked, waving the photograph.

He explained that 'the twin' is a reflection of Creepy Neighbour in the big mirror adjacent to his bed. 'That's why there's two of him,' he said, showing me my own reflection in our mirror.

Enthusiasm was getting the better of me. I'd been over-excited since finding a gallery interested in my show, and being given a lottery grant for 'materials' - more equipment from the Spy Shop.

My husband handcuffed me to the bed so that I wouldn't be tempted to go out again and take more pictures.

At dawn, as I was sleeping, arms bound above my head, Creepy Neighbour was taken away by the fraud squad.

There's a hole in my show now. I could hire someone to be Creepy? But it wouldn't be the same. Authentic creepiness can't be calculated.

It had started as a joke.

The joke became a game. Something to amuse me while James was away working on a secret project, in the Middle East or Eritrea or wherever he goes; and you were sulking with me.

'You never do anything,' you said, dismissively. And I thought, I'll show him, Mr full of himself fucking Director. Art isn't about how many millions you have in the bank, it's about risk. About how it affects the audience. How it changes you.

Ok, I was trying to impress you. To prove that I'm the cleverest, the funniest, the coolest. I'm not just a woman with an accent who's somebody's wife.

The neighbour caught my eye, tiptoeing past my window carrying large black bin bags in the middle of the night.

He was nearby. Available to be photographed in the garden, or car park, or sauna, sweating in his tight purple shorts. Sullenly lost in himself, head hung in the humidity, unaware of me.

After he was arrested, I was at a loose end. I went to the police station to make enquiries.

'Is he your father, Miss?' the policeman asked.

'Sort of,' I replied. He didn't believe me, but they are trained to be suspicious. It's not that I'm a bad liar.

'We can hold him for 24 hours,' the policeman explained. 'But that doesn't mean we will.'

Outside the police station, sun shining on the pollution, a poster caught my eye. So I got into a cab and went to the gallery. That's as good a place as any to kill time until his release. I'd like to have the stamina to sit outside the station and snap him as he emerges, but I lack the staying power for a Starbucks stakeout. I'd never make it as a paparazzi.

A line of Japanese girls waited in single file behind a cardboard box.

Orientals find queuing erotic. Giggling in excitement, they were dying to peer at something inside the box. A few minutes eavesdropping in the swarm of art tourists established what they were waiting to examine.

Half of me wanted to wait in line with them. Half of me felt too ridiculous. That's the curse of intelligence. The logical brain cancels out the impulsive emotions, leaving you in intellectual purgatory.

The left brain at war with the right brain. The one you love in competition with the one you used to love.

What would you think if you caught me in a queue to sniff an artist's knickers? Like I care what you, with your dimbo girlfriend and refusal to save me, think.

Anyway it's fascinating, the appeal of trash art. It lingers in your head like a predictable pop song. Singing along all day, out of tune, as long as nobody important is listening. Or like one of your movies - hook the audience in the first thirty seconds, you always say. Seduce and destroy. Or forget it.

It was like buying a blue car to match the ocean, then realising everyone has one.

Suddenly the artist's emotive face was everywhere, watching me, daring me. Her face changes for the worse when she smiles. She isn't too clever. Allowing the competitive girls in the gallery to think, I could be her. Everybody has neurotic fears, ripe for sexploitation.

I could have done that, art voyeurs say to themselves, as they sneak into the gallery to examine her work. The ideas are obvious and simple.

But you didn't do it. She did.

Everyone secretly wants to be an artist.

They mean a successful artist - a star. The intellectual credibility of a writer combined with the royalties of a rock star. To be worshipped, to be visible, to become 'real'. The fantasy of having pain obliterated by fame. Maybe tricking death with the illusion of immortality!

But that's not the whole story. Being visible contains the accompanying desire to be invisible. To be free.

'You can't live without dreams,' Great-aunt Tatiana said.

But can you live with them? The most common fantasy of love is murder. Love and death are sometimes the same thing.

I got home from the gallery at sunset, checked with Elvis - Creepy isn't back in the building - and unlocked the three deadlocks, admitting myself to my cool, clean space.

Everything is ivory - a virginal crack between purgatory and paradise. The air's scented with yellow roses you sent before your sulk started. Decayed around the edges; they smell ugly and unhappy like a woman who's not quite beautiful anymore.

The pale carpet tempted me to spill a glass of red

wine. The phone rang. I picked it up. Nobody there.

I switched on the television. Robbie Williams was having therapy on a chat show. 'Next year,' Robbie said, with a straight face, 'I'm going to take some time off and ask Rob what Rob wants to do next.'

Suddenly I have the answer.

Creepy Neighbour can't be depended on to appear as the centrepiece of my show. Any minute, he could be taken off again in a dawn raid. Arrested for the murder and mutilation of the woman who isn't his wife. But it doesn't matter. I have another, better, subject for me.

One I identify with, adore, and almost understand. Dislike, distrust, and leave out in the rain.

I started watching...my self.

First I changed the name. A hardship, when you are attached to your name. But my husband owns our name, and he's committed to secrecy.

After trying a few names that didn't feel right, I decided on Vivien Lash. The retro Vivien coupled with the sexy Lash. This new name grabs attention at the hairdressers, imprinted on my spiritually dayglo AmEx card.

Then I put Vivien Lash in a Lolita wig, for no particular reason. Remember the moment in *Blue Velvet* when Isabella Rossellini takes off her wig? It sticks in your mind.

'Why was she wearing a wig?' the voyeur with me asked. An ugly wig at that, sitting like a hat on her large, inherited head.

Ignore the question. Lick my Choc Ice. Who cares why? It's dark. Watch the movie. Old movies are impossible to abandon after midnight.

He became offended, wanted to leave. Some people think there's an answer for everything. They want to control the details as well as the plot, to reinvent the surface to suit their fantasy. And as they sit in the dark holding their breath, they change the end to a reassuring finish that makes it possible to forget the movie as soon as the lights come back on.

Vivien Lash's wig is long and straight and smooth, blue-black like the polluted night in Shanghai. A little tight, it tugs on the corners of her almond-shaped eyes, giving her a Chinese smile.

She has a future but not a past.

As a finishing touch, I decide Vivien Lash is a girl who never wears knickers. Then change my mind.

Where would I be without my scarlet silk pants hand-stitched by a dwarf in Shenzhen? Where would the dwarf be without his job? His despair breeding at night like my husband's secrets, a fungus covering his soul.

Love Always Spies

Elvis the porter invites Vivien Lash to join him in the Private Dick business. We can spy on Creepy Neighbour and catch him out when he gets up to his tricks.

'He'll get the full chocolate drop if he harms you, Miss, Elvis will see to it.'

Elvis is not really a porter, he has Big Plans and a wardrobe full of the other Elvis' clothes, including the jumpsuit he died in, which he bought with insurance money when his mother – sad as sin it was – passed to the Other Side.

'Who sold you the suit?'

Elvis looks behind to check no one's eavesdropping.

'Elvis is sworn to secrecy, Miss, but I can reveal that the King was buried in his smalls.'

The other Elvis's underwear probably wasn't that small, but I don't want to think about a bloated corpse's pants.

'I'm at Gracelands on all the big occasions, Miss,

like the day Elvis married Priscilla.'

Elvis got married in Vegas, but I don't want to spoil the fun.

'The King isn't dead you know, he faked it. All you need is a body and some Sellotape.' The other Elvis saw him when he peeked in the kitchen window last time he went to Gracelands.

'Was he eating a cheeseburger?'

'No he was standing there all alone, Miss, looking out at me.'

'What's the Sellotape for?'

Elvis taps his nose. 'Top secret, Miss.'

We sit in the gloom of my kitchen, drinking coffee with drowning cinnamon sticks, plotting our peeping tom larks.

'Is that your dad?' Elvis asks, looking at the picture on the wall by the fridge.

'It's Stanley Kubrick.'

'He looks like you,' Elvis says, not wanting to lose face. 'He could be your father.'

Stanley looks nothing like me on account of being a fat, swarthy man and me being a thin, white girl if glimpsed quickly in moonlight. But I let it go. How many people actually look like their father anyway? And Elvis is impossible to argue with on account of him being retarded, stubborn and unable to stop talking.

Elvis gives me the white Marilyn dress, the very one she wore in *The Seven Year Itch*, according to the man in the pub who sold it to him.

'Change into this, Miss, and you will surely be able to tempt Mr Creepy.'

'To do what?'

'You *know*.'

'I don't, as it goes.'

'To do the unspeakable. Then we can get him arrested.'

Creepy has put in a written complaint about Elvis peering in his bedroom window, so it's in his interest to have him arrested again. He doesn't care whether it's for murdering his wife, raping me, or double parking outside the steam room.

'I will of course be in the bushes the entire time with a torch at your service,' Elvis reassures me. Maybe the white dress will blow up, revealing white pants like the ones I flashed in Venice when I was 13.

Elvis does the cakewalk, cementing our bargain. The dress smells of Chanel No 5 and white trash sweat. Maybe he hired it from Angel Costumes? It's possible there never was a man, a pub, or an insurance policy. He tells enough lies to confuse a priest.

'Everything would have been different, Miss, if Elvis had married Marilyn.'

As I catwalk down the garden path in the *Itch* get-up, willing to make a fool of myself for Art, Elvis stage whispers from his bush, 'Don't worry, Mr Creepy will get nowhere near your turnpike.'

Buggery needs a beach and there are worse things than being raped, try telling that to Olga Borga. I haven't thought about her for years. Walking up and down the path, tempting fate, reminds me of the little victim who didn't stand a chance.

Nobody wanted to sit next to her on the bus. She smelled of wet pants and fear past its sell-by-date. Nobody would share a room with her so she had her own room with one bed for her and another for opportunity. We'll always have Venice.

Venice

My first run in with art was in Venice, wearing a scarlet sundress.

'You look like a sculpture,' the man said. He was lying on the cool steps of San Marco, taking pictures of my knickers, the glare of the sun stopping him from seeing up my skirt. I was wearing white panties and no bra.

In those days I always wore white underwear. Now I'm addicted to Chinese silk knickers. They don't come in white, the colour of death in China.

When I picked up the man in San Marco I hadn't been to Venice before. I was seduced by the smell of Catholicism and the canal. Water is God's tranquilliser, or the devil's bath depending on which side of the bridge you're sighing.

'Do you want to take me for ice-cream?' I asked, lifting up my red dress, wiping my sunglasses on the hem, to give him a better view of my pants.

The blond American tourist was tall when he stood up. He had two cameras and a sweaty smell wafting off his chest. I can't remember his name but vividly recall the creases around his eyes.

He could have been 35, or a badly preserved 28. Someone who lies in the high noon sun without sunblock. A risktaker, but not a heartbreaker. Heartbreakers have dark hair and don't come from the Midwest.

He followed me into Florians. We sat in the shade, sharing a chocolate leather banquette. I ordered coffee brandy ice-cream. Who knows what we talked about? I kicked off my sandals and massaged his thigh with my foot, proud of my Choosy Cherry toe paint. That's what you do in Italy, or maybe I'd seen it in a Claudia Cardinale movie.

Out of the corner of my eye, as I spooned ice-cream into the American's mouth, I saw Darko Novak running through the pigeons towards us. His right hand raised, he was pointing at me, shouting something I couldn't hear.

The American didn't see my teacher until he was upon us.

'This child is 12,' Darko said to the man, whose face had gone red. Sunburn catching up with him, or embarrassment at Darko's loud accusing tone?

'13,' I corrected.

'She never told me!' the man protested.

'You never asked,' I replied, spooning the remains of the ice-cream into my own mouth when he refused his turn. The brandy was making me drunk.

'She's not like any 13 year old I've met,' the man said, making Darko angrier.

'She's in Venice on a school trip!' he shouted.

Darko had applied for funds to bring a group of first years to Venice to study modern art, not realising that the art Biennale isn't on every year. He was a biology teacher after all.

The oddball sewing teacher present as our female chaperone pretended to be an art addict. There was a rumour that her and Darko had brought us to Venice as a beard for their activities. What these activities may be caused endless speculation about knitting needles and Bunsen burners.

We realised we were wrong when he was arrested for being a paedophile. In retrospect it seems odd that our mothers, neurotic women who constantly warned about 'bad men', allowed us to roam wild in the care of a biology teacher with a shiny bald head and steel-rimmed spectacles.

I could say that he bore a passing resemblance to Creepy Neighbour, but I'd be lying. Or allowing art to reshape memory.

A biology teacher who had that very summer in the school variety show directed a group of teens called the Fur Bikinis who were trained in his hut to do a karaoke pole dance to Serge Gainsbourg's *Je t'aime*. The pole we danced around was invisible, but that didn't stop us frotting our pelvises forward and making porno noises.

This show was performed, to loud applause, in the school gymnasium. The headmaster insisted that for the next performance the Fur Bikinis wear not the fur bikinis Darko had made for us but regulation black bathing suits. We stormed off in a trum, refusing to dance under censorship.

Darko took pictures of us in the forbidden fur bikinis, hanging them around the biology hut in what must have been a cry for help. A stop me while there's still time plea to the authorities. But nobody did, so we went to Venice and Olga Borga was buggered.

This wasn't exposed until years later. We had left school and been replaced by other 13 year olds on the school trip; switched from Venice to Split, because Darko and the sewing teacher 'needed a beach'.

Who knows what the educational purpose of this trip was? Bet it beat weekends in Auschwitz, red raw from the wind, buttoning up your coat tight to the throat then feeling itchy like everything's your fault after all.

I went to the Biennale with my husband.

A real holiday, not a work trip, though of course he made contact with the Russians who pop up on yachts everywhere it's expensive. He likes to keep his hand in, spy on the other team, or just meet them for drinks.

Between parties, we drank Prosecco on the roof of the borrowed palazzo, talked about Titian, smiled at the stars, made jokes about the fat girl who leered at him in San Michele.

Sexual betrayal was a joke between us then. Ha fucking ha.

'Tell me a story,' he said, in the pause between sunset and darkness as we sat on the edge of the roof.

'I don't know any stories.'

'A story about you. When you were young.'

'I've forgotten being young.'

'How did you escape?'

'You know that story.'

'Did you really walk?'

'Sometimes I had to swim.'

'I can never be sure if you're telling the truth.'

'I worked as a waitress in a cocktail bar, that much is true.'

I walked to Trieste in the wrong shoes. I kept on and on walking. I took a boat, a train. I hitchhiked. Sometimes I forgot to pretend to be a boy.

I'd always wanted to escape. To flee the country, see the world. Wake up with a new name and a new hair colour and a heart that's almost the same.

'You can do anything when you're clever,' Great-aunt Tatiana told me before she tucked me in and kissed me Goodnight.

It wasn't all fun.

I had a job strangling chickens in Bangkok, blood in my fringe and behind my fingernails in the picture I have still in my head. In Hanoi, I sold custard apples in the street, hoping for the best. And in Kuala Lumpur, where the jungle eats its way into the city, I worked as a hostess in a tea shop.

Walking around South East Asia maybe, thinking of you. A future escape I hadn't invented yet, one I imagined even before we'd met.

'Tell me another story,' he said, holding my hand in the dark, watching the moon burn.

Later, after dinner, when he'd been irritated by the presence of someone at another table, we got lost in the dark on our way home.

'You go that way if you want to,' he barked, as we backtracked down an alley, crossing one canal too many, the palazzos all looking the same.

And suddenly it was easy to dislike him. The small gestures are important. Details that make you hate or love.

'You look like an Italian movie star in that dress,' you told me. My husband, when I wore the same dress tonight, said with a laugh, 'You've been eating too much pasta.'

Suddenly I wanted to kill him, wanted to die. Emotions change in an instant. There's no going back, until the next time.

He thinks I have erased every trace because nothing shows on the surface. Imperfections. Sadness. Doubt.

'Nothing marks you,' he said as we drank Aperol in the movie star bar in Cannaregio.

'Nothing?'

'Nothing ugly.'

'You will have to kill me,' I said, checking my reflection in the dark window, an old habit I've almost outgrown, 'if you want to erase everything.'

He touched my face with the cool side of his hand.

His skin is soft.

'Can you trust a man who works with his brain?' Great-aunt Tatiana asks. Can you trust a man who doesn't?

'Not you,' he said, 'nothing can spoil you.'

He's wrong. It's with me everywhere - the memory of being poor, the feeling of being trapped, the desire to escape.

And when I escaped, I found him.

We had a nice time in Venice, even though he took me there out of guilt, to make up for the money he had spent on third world romances the previous winter.

It's not about sex, it's about making them fall in love.

Before you turned up at Cipriani's, laughing at the coincidence, your skinny girlfriend and sour assistant in tow; we took daisies to Diaghilev on the Island of the Dead. I walked barefoot over the weeds on Ezra Pound's grave, allowing the lizards to kiss my flesh.

'Put your shoes back on,' my husband barked. 'I have something for you.' And he took the black pearls out of his pocket. A man who gives you pearls wants to strangle you, according to Great-aunt Tatiana. But women like me don't get strangled in sunlight.

We escaped San Michele and got drunk in Peggy Guggenheim's garden where she's buried with her dogs. We walked to the church Nicolas Roeg used in *Don't Look Now*, past the shop where Stanley Kubrick had the masks made for *Eyes Wide Shut*.

'It's not reality, it's a photograph of reality,' Stanley

used to say, when he was alive.

And when Stanley died, Nicky Kidman called Steve Spielberg in tears. 'And we flew over and buried Stanley in his backyard,' Spielberg said, emotional in the way only a man obsessed with childhood can be. Now when I see Kidman can-canning in *Moulin Rouge*, I imagine her wielding a spade.

My feet were covered in blisters from my pink Choos when we reached the cool dark of the church. I stepped barefoot across the stone, healing. Lighting a candle, I spied my reflection in the gilt candelabra. A woman with wide hips and a flabby waist kneeled forward, joining me in the mirror like a warning.

'You will have three children,' she whispered with conviction, counting the beads at her throat. 'All that's gold does not glister.'

'What did she say?' my husband asked, outside in the sun.

'Her son's in the mafia and will have you murdered for a small stipend.'

That made him laugh. He trusts me. His confidence is almost touching. But can you ever trust anyone to stay in character? Everything's a game and a game needs a loser.

Why do I have to kill him?

Why can't we just get a divorce? He would bring me home. Marry me again.

Is it something to do with concealment? I almost understand. His heart is hidden, protected. Mine is exposed.

He will never let me go. So I have to let him go.

If I don't kill him, I might be tempted to forgive him.

Drinking bellinis on the terrace at Cipriani, we talked about the school trip. Boys weren't allowed. It was only the girls who got to go to Venice for reasons that weren't obvious until later.

When he disappeared from the table, too impatient to wait for a waiter; on impulse I called Tasha, my best friend when I was 13. The memory of running naked through the snow with her, to the sauna in the woods, is crucial to my Polaroid of childhood. Her children now go to the school that we used to. She is always home ironing pants and looking for things lost.

'Hello,' she said, sounding bored.

'Guess where I am?!'

Tasha was overcome with excitement. She almost wet herself.

'My pelvic floor muscles have been weak since having my last cherub,' she explained when she had caught her breath.

Her excitement was not merely the surprise of hearing from a lost friend. She had Big News and couldn't get over the coincidence. Life is full of them, it's only in art that they aren't allowed.

She told me about Darko Novak's arrest.

'He's been at it for years. Do you remember Olga

Borga? The one glued to his lap.'

Rows of faceless first years bent over the biology bench popped into my mind. The image creates a negative on my visual memory of a sight I never witnessed.

Against my will, I couldn't help wondering if he'd used Vaseline when he buggered Olga Borga? Was anal penetration a kindness, making sure she didn't get pregnant? A precaution so that she wouldn't give the show away by turning into two people? A way of avoiding looking her in the eye?

Or just Darko Novak's preference.

But there are worse things than being raped.

How the fuck would I know? I have not been raped.

'Yet,' Elvis's voice shouts in my ear.

In England, teenage rape is another word for a night out.

Tracey Emin was 'broken into' when she was 13.

'As a woman I'll be criticised for saying this,' she confessed on Radio 4, 'but there are worse things than being raped.'

In Margate, where she lived, breaking into young girls was part of the culture. A tribal thing. What else is there to do at the seaside? And can you imagine the humiliation of not being picked?

At least it got her out of Margate. She made her tent and lay in it, the names of 102 fuck buddies on the wall. She didn't need to make her bed.

Cashing in on cruel youth, the trivial almost erasing the profound - like a kiss stealing your soul - until she spoils the joke. Now that she's rich and famous, she admits she's only had 'about 15 lovers'.

Does the hideous word 'lovers' include the men who raped her? Is it 5 boyfriends: 10 rapists. 10 boy-friends: 5 rapists. Who knows? She can't be expected to keep score. It's art after all. And she isn't poor anymore.

As a poor girl, she must have been pathetic playing the part of Mad Tracey from Margate. But as a successful artist, being a little crazy doesn't hurt.

You get to be drunk on TV, boast about your abortions, and take your false teeth out in public. You don't get raped anymore, you'd probably charge - or turn it into an installation. Emotional copyright is clear-cut. It's your life. Why not charge admission, so long as somebody wants to buy a ticket?

When you're really in love you whisper. You don't cheapen it by talking about it, using it as therapy, or converting into profitable art. That's like charging your boyfriend for sex.

Or is it? As Martin Scorsese says, 'Movies are the memories of our lifetimes.' Whose life should an artist exploit if not their own? Some people are just better at reinvention. Truth, when it's overdressed, sounds like a lie.

And mad Tracey's right. There are worse things than being raped. There's always something worse.

I escaped from the seaside too, but not by being raped. I ran away from my fate, the poverty of potato-faced ancestors, the lack of imagination.

Being poor is worse than being raped. It lasts longer. It's more mundane. Being poor poisons you slowly. Rape at its best is quick and bestial. It's common to fantasise about it.

But nobody fantasises about being poor. Who lies on their bed daydreaming about having no money? Being poor for too long makes it impossible to believe in dreams anymore. Even when they happen.

But there are things you are allowed to say out loud. And others you are supposed to keep to yourself.

When I saw my husband coming back, I hung up on Tasha.

'Who were you talking to?'

'No one.'

'I saw you.'

'No one important.'

We started a conversation about football. Footballers have something sexy about them, despite being ugly and stupid. They have huge fan clubs. Suffer their fifteen seasons of fame then move into the world of owning failed nightclubs. Drinking the profits, perversely addicted to spray tan and bad hair in themselves and others.

Footballers rape girls. They don't get raped. Except maybe by each other in the shower.

What is a rape fantasy?

Fantasy is something you don't really want to happen. Rape is a fantasy of desire. Imagine a man who can arouse the desire in you for him to rip off your dress and fuck you. The possibility of this happening, not the reality. You don't want to meet him on a dark night in Shanghai.

Rape is a failure of seduction. I don't need to try it to know that it would be degrading. I have never been murdered but know that I don't want to be. I'd rather kill than be killed.

Last year we went to visit a Turkish prison with Baroness somebody or other.

My husband was writing a report, and the Baroness was having a good sneer at Turkey's human rights record. Wives have to park their personalities in the hotel safe for the duration of the jolly, or I would have pointed out her pleasure.

I'd rather sit at a pool with a cocktail than smell other peoples' shit. (Who wouldn't? Her!) But Baroness Butt-Plug insisted that I join them.

'Your poor wife will be bored all alone,' she said to James, like I couldn't hear her.

The heat made the smell worse and the men looked at me with dead, frightened eyes. Had I been brought here to tempt them?

No. They're chained. Specially for our visit? It made Baroness Butt-Plug's day. She made a, 'Tit Tat Tut,' sound with her tongue as we paraded through the stinky hole.

The prison governor was affronted. He mistook the sound her lips were making for something sexual. Maybe he's right? Desire is at once specific and indefinable. Sometimes it's a secret even from your self.

Had any of these men been raped?

Probably. But when she asked, they denied it. Who wants to admit they have been somebody's bitch?

Elvis's friend Bernie had a bad time in prison and he wasn't even in Turkey. He was punished for being 'a bit different'.

I wonder how Darko Novak is enjoying prison? I doubt if he will be picked to be anally raped. If Darko hadn't rushed across San Marco through the pigeon shit to rescue me, would I have been raped by the American tourist?

Or seduced him into paedophilia with another flash of my snow-white Lolita pants? Or skipped away after scoffing the expensive ice-cream to meet my friends as arranged by the Vaporetto, taking my purity with me?

Darko protected the school from scandal until it was time for his starring role in his own sordid story.

As we set off on the school trip, Olga Borga, overweight and spotty, was sitting alone on the bus taking us to the airport. Prime meat for a paedophile to pick on.

Beauty protects children. Stand out too much and the pervert is afraid to come into your spotlight.

Darko had forgotten something. The coach driver stopped outside his house and Darko ran up the ver-tiginous steps leading to the front door.

His son, a blond boy around our age watching from the window, made eye contact with me before disappearing behind the curtain. In the split second he looked at me, I could feel his shyness.

His father collected the forgotten camera - a spare, just in case - and came back out to the coach, taking his seat at the front.

'That boy never leaves the house,' he said, to no one and everyone.

What happened to him? What happened to me? I grew up to be a wife. An artist. An escape artist.

Before I met James, I was a dancer. Then I couldn't dance anymore so I tried to sing. But that's a different story, an old story, even its memories almost invisible now.

The sun's almost up.

Creepy Neighbour hasn't been tempted to come out in the dark and rape me. Elvis is snoring under the bush.

And I can hear my phone ringing. It stops and starts again almost immediately. You must really want to talk to me tonight.

Sex Crimes in the Bush

Elvis is upset that parading me through the garden as Marilyn didn't tempt Creepy Neighbour to do the unspeakable.

Looking strange doesn't make him a sexual deviant. Raping his neighbour probably just isn't on his list. The poor mook is probably impotent.

'Maybe he just doesn't fancy me,' I told Elvis, when we met in the boiler room to discuss our failed surveillance operation Sex Crimes in the Bush.

'We need one of them fans,' Elvis said, depressed. He's off duty incognito today so not dressed in his sparkly Vegas jumpsuit. A bit of glitter turns him into a different man. 'To blow up your skirt.'

The wind is my enemy.

'No merkin, no wind machine,' I said, confusing Elvis. Merkin is such a fabulous word I drop it into every conversation.

The next time I'm insulted or delighted, I'm planning to shout, 'You twisted merkin!'

A merkin in case you don't know is a pubic wig.

A fur muff thong favoured by women who've had a bikini wax too many. Merkins come in different shades of fake mink but in only one size: small. Currently sold in Soho but before long they will be on the shelves of every supermarket.

'You will have to show more commitment, Miss,' Elvis said, gathering his dignity, 'if we are going to make a success of this here Dick business.'

This story amuses you.

'When we're talking on the phone, I can never tell when you're lying,' you say. As if truth's always transparent when you look someone in the eye.

You want me to tell you stories, reveal myself. You have that in common with James. Imagining I know the secret, that I keep the real me hidden behind my mascara and lip gloss.

'What were you like…before?'

'Before I became a private detective?'

'Before you met him.'

You mean James. I could pretend I think you mean Elvis. But I'm not in the mood to annoy you tonight.

'What am I like now?'

'You're beautiful…but strange.'

I'm as narcissistic as the next person, seeking my identity in the mirror where my evil twin stares back at me.

'I never know what you're thinking.'

Clarifying the picture ruins the illusion. But you earn a living polishing surfaces and don't want to admit there isn't always something more interesting underneath.

'I'm me when I'm with you.' This pleases you.

'The real you.' All of them are real. All of them are me. The girl who escaped on a boat, a train, a magic carpet, and kept looking back over her shoulder in a paparazzi pose.

'What are you scared of?'

'Everything.'

'Do you think if I see the real you I won't love you anymore?'

I smile without replying, pretend your pop psychology isn't predictable. The game goes like this. Good me and bad me. Clean me and dirty me. Your me and his me. Imagining I'm an imposter, pretending to be my self. Except I know that all of them are the real me.

Silence disturbs you.

'Are you still there?'

'One day you will see the real me and think I'm one of the fakes.'

The relationship between reality and illusion isn't complex. Sometimes they appear to be the same because they are.

'Tell me a story,' you insist, used to getting your own way.

'I don't know any stories.'

'How did you get your scar?'

'I was born with it.'

'It looks new.'

'Only when it rains. Or I'm close to water.' Water

reminds me of Vivien Leigh as a ballerina in *Waterloo Bridge*. The Thames gets her in the end. I love water more than dry land.

'It's not raining now, why don't I come and get you? We can just leave. Now. Tonight. Forget about James fucking Bond.'

'What about my show?'

You don't take my work seriously. Why would you? I spy on strange men for a living. You get paid £3,000,000 for 30 seconds work any time you feel like dirtying your hands with advertising money.

'We'll come back for that.'

But I can't come back. Escaping means never going home.

'Have you forgotten already what happened in Havana?'

But that's a story you don't want to be reminded of. You hang up. But you'll phone back in a minute. Silence gets on your nerves.

I don't need you to call me, just to be out there somewhere in the night, obsessing about me.

Havana

I could never love a man who loved someone else, or a city he saw first without me.

We're on the roof of the Hotel Nacional in Havana, your commercial's finished and I'll be surprised if I make the final cut. The client will ask what the fuck I'm doing in an advert for dark beer.

We sat watching fleas dance in rotting upholstery, your camera in and out of your pocket like a gangster's gun. James never allows his photograph to be taken except for one of his passports.

'Photographing someone is a sign of love,' you said, pleased with your obsession. You're a professional after all, and don't own the original.

'Did you read that in Vogue?' You first saw me in a magazine. You tore out the promising young artist and stuck her on your wall.

'Ha fucking ha.' You saw my photograph and fell in love. That's your story.

'I hate having my photograph taken.'

'Models always say that.' You moved backwards,

dangerously close to the edge of the roof as you focused on your shot. One more step and you'll fall.

'I'm not a model, I'm an artist.'

'Every picture tells a story.'

'The camera makes me cry.'

'You mean the camera never lies.'

'That's a big fucking lie. You digitally alter everything.'

'Improvements are a different kind of truth.' You're trying to sound profound again. I prefer you trivial, but it's touching that you make the effort to impress me.

'Everybody beautiful reminds me of you. Yet nobody looks like you.'

A woman's intelligence is ignored when she's beautiful; a man is underestimated if he's rich and good-looking. You put the camera down and touched my face.

'Nobody looks like you,' I said. But it's a lie. You look like a younger, taller, less intense version of James; a good cover version.

Suddenly it's dark. We're an hour older. The minute you are born you start to cry.

I'm spinning the world, one of your props, the globe almost falls off the table.

'I'll take you anywhere.'

'There's nowhere I want to go.'

'Pick somewhere. We can...escape.'

'I like it here.'

'You're right. Here's perfect.'

The stars spying on us, the scent of frangipani and bougainvillea bothering my nostrils. Ingredients for a voodoo love potion like the one you bought me for a laugh. Dead flowers stink.

My black pearls are strangling me, making me too hot, but they sulk when I put them in the safe. You take them off, hide them in your pocket.

'You will have to strip search me to get them back,' you said, backing away recklessly towards the edge again, just out of reach; when his face appeared on the roof.

He was just passing, come to take me home, something about a meeting in Mexico.

'Show off,' you muttered. His youthful good looks shock you. You can't stop yourself from scrutinising him as he walks closer.

'It's his job. He goes everywhere.' With everyone.

James barely glanced at you. He touched my throat and said, 'You're not wearing your pearls.'

I stood between you, intending to make a formal introduction. The muscles in your stomach are clenched so hard I'm almost sick.

That is how it will always be.

He will come and take me home. He's cleverer than you. You're richer than him. He was the star of the football team, you were never picked. You didn't want to play anyway.

Your sulk had started already, while the three of us

sat on the roof having one last mojito.

James raised an eyebrow, but ordered one anyway. I don't normally like sugary drinks. I couldn't finish it with him watching. I pushed it away, like it was intended as irony all along.

The tension in your shoulders, poised for a punch in the back as you turned and walked to the edge of the roof, was painful to witness.

I want you to turn around, to say something; look him in the eye at least.

But you don't so he takes me home.

Tainted Love

A return journey is different from an outward journey.

The suspense of travelling somewhere is replaced with the resolution of going home.

On the way back from Havana, my husband sat beside me instead of you. We look good together, an attractive couple sharing easy silence. He allows me to stare at the clouds, never pesters me about what I'm thinking.

I have a book unopened on my knee about the dead popstar Billy Mackenzie. The perfume James bought in Babylon infuses the air between us. His beauty offends you, that much was clear from the look you gave me before retreating to your room.

He doesn't lean into me, like you did on the outward journey, whispering in my blue diamond ear. Desiring me with your eyes. Following me as I walked to the back of the cabin. Seeing me everywhere in your imagination at least. He loves me in a different way.

'It's your funeral,' your text message said.

I haven't deleted it yet.

We changed at Milan, making a picnic of the journey with blue cheese for him and Gucci shoes for me. You don't buy me presents. Except silly things like a cool voodoo doll with a dirty white dress and a love potion which doubles up as poison.

'Kill or cure,' you said, passing me the pouch of toxic powder. I've never understand that expression or wanted to.

You find money embarrassing, are reluctant to look like a show off splashing out on expensive gifts, trying to buy my love.

This instinct is imbedded in you because you make the money yourself, vats and vats of it every year. You despise it. It embarrasses you. The last thing you want is to be considered materialistic.

But I love money! It makes me feel safe. You will never understand. Money can be controlled more than love or revolution or the warrior planet Mars, crowding closer to Earth this century than it's ever done before.

You think I'm joking? Check your ephemeris (all you fashionable young things secretly have one). The sky, along with the evening news, seems to be telling us, *It's your turn next*.

Writing things down is dangerous.

I know that. So why am I doing it?

Is it a desire to confess my sins before I commit them? Am I hoping he'll read my diary, catch me red-handed, put a stop to my plans?

He has to go out, an important meeting.

I sat on our bed in my white silk pyjamas, watching him in the mirror as he checked my phone. You won't call me, not tonight.

You're drunk already, telling yourself I'm a waste of time. I've forgotten if flying home made me a day older or a day younger. If you're awake or asleep, or in the limbo of jealous insanity in between.

You want me because you can't have me. That old trick!

'If you were blonde,' James said, playing with my dayglo white foot, 'you'd be invisible.'

He's in the shower.

I hear his phone ring. Walking towards the sound, I see his phone carelessly abandoned on our bed. It's not ringing.

I pick it up, hold it in my hand, walk towards the sound of the rings. Tiptoe past his bathroom, into his dressing-room; warmer.

His spare phone's ringing in his safe. Do phones retain memories of evil? Do they know when you're telling lies?

The other phone's in my hand, silent.

There are no new messages. Everything has been deleted from his Inbox. Except this one message, which came four minutes after he went into the shower.

Can't wait.

He dragged me home, spoiling my fun, and now he's spitting on my heart again with his secret meetings.

He only listens when I stop talking. Who wants to be loved by the undiscriminating? Who wants to be loved.

Sins of the heart are worse than sins of the flesh.

Instead of committing adultery, I'd committed a sin of the heart - continuing to want something I refused to take. Tempted to fall asleep in your arms forever. Determined to stay awake and face Vivien Lash in the mirror.

Spiders take on the colour of their surroundings. Adultery is for the bourgeoisie. I've been with these people so long I'm starting to act like them. It was never my intention to assimilate. I prided myself on uniqueness, recognising the illusion.

I'm leading a double life. By night a conformer, during the day a dabbling radical.

Betrayal is a cliché. But murder is nice and clean.

I sat on top of the bed in my yellow silk pyjamas.

The white ones are unlucky. It's easy to take them off. I'm not invisible anymore.

I checked my face in the mirror, opened the book about Billy Mackenzie. One day at Billy's house his dad brought in a cake and Billy said, 'That cake is like your auntie's hat.'

That image kept replaying in my mind, another memory of something I didn't witness, as James came out of the bathroom.

'What are you reading?' he asked.

'A book,' I said, flicking to the end, where Billy kills himself and goes to sleep forever in the dog basket.

He looked at the cover. 'You changed your PJs.'

'I spilled something.'

'What?'

'Chicken blood.'

'It's important,' he said, 'or I wouldn't go out.'

'Have fun,' I said.

'As if,' he said. 'Don't wait up.'

I can't wait any longer.

I decided to kill him in our bedroom.

Antique white walls, matching carpet, soft under my bare feet. A feeling of defencelessness. White lilies in their silver vase soothing us to sleep. Great-aunt Tatiana always warned me never to sleep in a room with white flowers of all things.

The poison caught my eye.

The stuff from the voodoo doctor, bought for a laugh, ha fucking ha. I stirred it into a glass of water, left it on the bedside table.

Should I swallow the poison, or leave it there in the dark for him to drink? Him or me?

I added some Rohypnol, just in case, crushing it up.

1 for fun, 2 for sleep, 10 so that we'll never meet again.

I woke up alive, surprised, sick, and started to cry.

'What's wrong, Baby?' James asked, putting his hand out in the dark to find me.

I locked myself in the bathroom and sent you a text message.

HELP

But I can't let you see me sick. I'll pretend it's a joke if you call me, concerned. Anyway you're still in Havana. Sulking, hating me, refusing to give in this time and make the first move.

Thinking about this gives me a headache. Headaches make me think of Charlotte Rampling who was born to have headaches.

In real life I insist on happy endings. Like Scott Fitzgerald said after paradise was lost, 'I don't care about truth, I just want some happiness.'

I don't want to be tortured. The right brain cancelling out the left brain until I'm erased. Stuck in the blind spot between dream and logic.

Just say no!

I've wasted enough time spying on strange men.

It didn't occur to me that a strange man might be spying on me.

Shanghai

Outside in the communal garden, the lights come on. My eyes adjust to the present tense.

The garden path is lit from below, like a stage. Creepy Neighbour lurches along it, the familiar slouch silhouetted against my window. Is he hiding something else in the bin; or just having a midnight stroll in the garden?

Moonlight captures his face. A face in decline, frozen with longing. For what?

He catches me watching. I don't bother ducking. He looks hopeful, pleading. He thinks I fancy him?!

Elvis still has his heart set on Creepy raping me. 'To prove he's a pure rotten to the core perv.' Providing Elvis with the opportunity to step out of his role of night porter and execute a daring *Taxi Driver* style rescue mission.

But I'm not playing. I'm bored with that game. Elvis is no Travis Bickle. And I'm the director of this show. I can have my happy ending?

The man opposite, the one who never leaves the

house, drops his grey curtain when I catch him peering across at me; watching me spy on Creepy.

People who never leave the house are usually locked in there dreaming of escape. Running away, never going home again. Going to the corner shop for a packet of cigarettes and catching a plane to freedom instead. That's the fantasy you're allowed to admit in daylight. Falling in love is the other one.

Murder is best kept for after midnight. Confined to the safety of your own mind where your subconscious is the only witness.

That's how murderers get caught. That need to confess their sins. The longing for absolution that's older than God.

The palm trees by my front door cast a shadow, like two sentries. Are they standing there for my protection, to keep me safe; or are they my guards, stationed to make sure I don't escape?

The phone rings, distracting me.

I lie down on my bed before answering. I know it's you before you speak.

'What are you wearing?' you ask, using your seductive voice.

'Underwear.'

'What colour?'

'The scarlet ones you bought me in Hong Kong.'

'Liar.'

'You're right, they're more Chinese red than scarlet. Closer to the colour of lipstick than blood.'

'You're not wearing any knickers. You're lying naked on your bed.'

Are you crouching behind the palm tree, looking in my window? Would that be art or peeping? Does love prevent voyeurism from being creepy? Or is spying on the one you love worse than watching your creepy neighbour alone in his bedroom?

'Are you watching me?'

'Of course, I spy on you every night.'

'I'm your installation?'

'No it's my new movie.'

'What's it called?'

'*Spying on Sexy Women.*'

You hesitate, I can feel you holding your breath.

'Do you want to run away to Shanghai with me?'

You sound shy, ashamed you couldn't hold out another hour at least before suggesting a new escape plan. But now we're not just running away, we're going somewhere. The general idea of escape has become a specific location.

'Shanghai,' I whisper into your ear.

I love the sound of that word. In Shanghai I'm a day older but ten times richer.

Gene Tierney in *The Shanghai Gesture* squandering her beauty in an opium den. Me in the elevator to the Glamour Bar with him. I saw his face first in a mirror.

Never fall in love with a man you first see in a mirror. Why didn't I listen to Great-aunt Tatiana when she was alive?

Standing side by side in the luminous sky coffin, he didn't speak until we were almost at the top floor.

'It's impossible to get a taxi when it rains here,' he said, and I noticed moisture on his eyelashes, unlikely to be mistaken for tears; and wondered why he didn't have his own driver? Except he does, but doesn't always want a witness to know where he's been.

'You sound like Sean Connery,' I said. And he laughed.

'Bond,' he said, 'James Bond.'

Shanghai is where he fell in love with me; where he saw me for the first time, walking towards the lift, and followed me.

'Where were you going?' I asked, as I watched his reflection in the window, unable for reasons I don't admit out loud to look him in the eye yet.

'I was looking for you, I just didn't know it.'

He went to make a telephone call but left his phone on the table. I picked it up. It felt hot. This was before I knew he was a spy, with his multiple passports and secret phones and girls who send their vulgar photograph, disturbing the silence.

He came back and caught me in the act.

'Practising my Shanghai Lil routine,' I said. 'It will take more than one man to break her.'

He laughed, taking his phone out of my hand, saying, 'My secrets are on the other one.'

His fingers were cold when they brushed against mine. And I like that. Cold and hard like marble, not warm and sticky like yours when you pawed me on the roof.

Many men loved Shanghai Lil, only one was loved in return. The brain is sometimes the tastiest part of an animal. A cup of blood is good for the heart.

Shanghai means revenge.

'Are you still there?'

'No.'

'What are you thinking about?'

'I was enjoying the silence.'

'You can do that in Shanghai.'

'Shanghai,' I whisper again. Even my voice betrays him.

'Run away with me,' you say, voice full of happiness and hope.

'Why would we run?'

'We can fly First Class.'

'You mean you don't have a Time Machine?'

'Would you love me more than him if I had a Time Machine?'

Is allowing yourself to be loved harder than loving? The subject or the object; the noun or the verb.

'Who says I love you?'

A party always has more than two. The one you love more, and the one who loves you more.

He'll never let me go.

Until death do us part?

Forever is what happens when I'm painting my toenails, waiting for electric blue to dry. Eternity is a place where somebody gets smothered.

'You love me. You just won't say it.'

'I have to go, there's someone at the door.'

You hang up without saying goodbye like they do in your movies.

Why do I have to fucking kill him?

Why can't I just get a divorce like a normal neurotic person instead of making these psychotic plans like a character from Greek tragedy?

Most girls leave their dolls under the bed when they run away from home. I arranged my toys in an aesthetic pile and burned them. My first installation?

I want to kill him.

It's tidy. Clean. Final. No temptation to forgive. If he doesn't exist, he can't hurt me again. He can't follow me and bring me home.

My rival is watching me, mocking me, staring me out.

She would know exactly what to do. She would have fucking done it by now.

She looks happy and sure of herself, safe inside her silver frame, sitting serenely on my dressing-table. Self-confident young cunt.

A plot twist has a single source in a movie, a moment revolutionises everything. Suddenly the light changes and nothing will ever be the same again.

In real life betrayal sneaks up on you, hiding under your fingernails, living under the bed along with a suitcase that's been too many places.

I turn the picture away from me, but now it's reflected in the mirror. My mythically perfect younger self can still see me. She's the one he married. The one he fell in love with. Does he love her more than me? Of course he does!

There's a ring at the door, or maybe it's my phone, hiding in the dark.

No message. No missed call.

I unlock the door, try to open it, remember the two bolts at the bottom; and I'm in my scarlet pants.

When I come back wearing my bathrobe the door is open. I never leave it open, even for a second. I must have?

Outside there's a single white lily waiting on the Chinese red doormat. The two palm trees act casual like they have witnessed nothing. Palm trees dislike living in England. They can't stand the weather.

The Middle

'There is no such thing as pointless violence.'
Martin Scorsese

Vivien Lash visited a witch in Hampstead, looking for the answer or even the fucking question.

Saturn is in my house of love and death. A heavy planet which creates merry hell then moves on to torture its next victims.

The witch explained that her interpretations are neutral, non-judgemental.

'Freud with a broomstick?'

'Jung with a black cat,' she replied, her poker face extending before my eyes. But, like Freud and Jung before her, she couldn't resist sneaking in a few hardcore subjective judgements.

'You,' she said to the table, 'are having a visit from the God of Hell soon.' Pointing at me, she shouted, 'There's no reason why you should go with him!'

'So...running away together's not a good idea?'

'It's more about a mental journey,' the witch explained, while mixing herbs for a banishment ritual. 'This guy here,' she said, pounding the table, 'isn't going anywhere. He has work to do on himself.'

She paused, staring at Vivien's navy blue eyelashes, the ones I attached with glue this morning. Mornings are blue and sunsets are scarlet. I wish I was 124 in an octagonal room contemplating Chinese red. I used to like looking in the mirror.

'This guy's a train wreck.'

'He loves me.'

'That's Neptune talking,' the witch, who is also an astrologer, insisted.

Astrology began in Babylon. In those days God enjoyed a brew. The blood of a newborn maybe with fresh lamb roasted on a spit in succulent sacrifice.

The banishment ritual didn't work. I didn't want it to.

'When Saturn leaves your sign this man will leave your orbit.' Her certainty is laughable. I'm not counting the days. I should have been.

'He is dangerous to you.'

'Which man?'

Is she talking about you, my husband, Creepy Neighbour? All three? I've not been paying attention. Distracted by the trees outside her window. Distracted by me.

'This one!' the witch shouted, staring into her Formica table. 'Pay attention or this won't work.'

I corrected my posture, made my face serious; but not too serious. She wasn't fooled.

'You may be wearing the right shoes,' she snorted, 'but you know nothing about magic.'

She made tea.

'I don't drink tea.'

'Drink it.' She watched as I pretended to sip.

'Ok,' I said, standing up, brisk and full of purpose. 'That was great! How much do I owe you?'

'Sit down,' she ordered, 'we're not finished with you yet.'

We?! Does the cat have plans for me next? My crumblie neighbour told me about a rapist cat who uses his paw because his penis is too small. I'd assumed she was havering.

The witch doesn't like the look of my solar horoscope.

'Someone is going to lose their head,' she said, staring alternately at her crystal ball and my teacup.

Suddenly I felt too ridiculous to ask for a magic potion. She was wearing me out with her sighs and stares. I wanted to leave, but didn't have the will to stand up again.

'There is betrayal in your chart,' she said, 'due to the pivotal position of Pluto.' She delivered this like a weather report, lurched forward to kick her cat, then asked, like it was a trick question, 'What day is today?'

'Tuesday,' I said, refusing a Topic from the big bin on the floor. She'd been offering me sweets from this selection of mini bars since I arrived.

'A dark secret will be revealed on Thursday,' the witch said.

Some people dislike secrets but they attract me. I don't fear sudden change. My husband's girlfriend – at least the one I've seen, who has a face like a whore's holiday – has given me absolution. A reason beyond my own desire, a justification accepted by some courts, to murder him.

This motive came at the right time, as I started to suspect that I'm incurably indecisive. Everyone sees me as a character in control of my destiny - except this witch, who reserves omnipotence for herself - but really I am hopeless at choices. What I'm good at is eliminating things I don't want to do. If this narrows the options down to one, a decision is no longer necessary.

'A secret of mine?' I asked. 'Or someone else's?'

The witch was irritated by these questions. 'I'm not a fortune teller,' she reminded me. Adding, 'Expect fireworks.'

She left me alone in the room with the cat. Bored, I delved into the bin of sweets, unwrapping a Topic. As I was about to put it in my mouth, the witch flew back in, screaming, 'You ate the last Topic!'

I haven't eaten it yet, but don't know the etiquette. Should I wrap it up and drop it back in the bin? Tell her to keep her merkin on? Remind her she's been goading me to eat chocolate since I arrived? Or just get the fuck out of her cave before I end up in a cauldron with the cat.

While I was dithering over a decision, she made one for me.

'I have urgent personal business to attend to,' she said, taking the Topic from my hand and *locking it in a drawer*. 'I will drive you home.'

'No need,' I said, watching her put the key in her purse. Thank fuck I didn't bite the Topic or she could do major voodoo on me.

'I'm afraid there is,' she said, 'you could be mugged at this time of night in this neighbourhood.'

We're in fucking Hampstead, and it's three in the afternoon. Arguing didn't seem appropriate. I got into her truck and fastened my seatbelt.

After driving for about 30 seconds, she parked her large vehicle in Flask Walk outside the writer Al Alvarez's house. The last man known to whiff Sylvia Plath's hair, as she ascended the stairs ahead of him a few days before suiciding.

'Wait here,' the witch told me, locking me in the truck.

Alvarez, who describes himself as a poker player who writes as a hobby, understands risk. Art and risk go hand in hand. Do I know him well enough to phone him and say, 'I'm locked in a witch's truck outside your door and I think she's going to murder me.'

And what could ancient Al do anyway? I doubt if he misspent his youth breaking into cars, he was too busy plotting suicide. He doesn't look the type to sledgehammer a windscreen, allowing me to crawl out.

The witch came flying back into the truck carrying a large box. She plonked it down on the seat between us.

I sneaked a look inside while she was screaming abuse at another driver. The box contained a big cake. Orange icing that could cause kidney failure in one bite. She caught me looking, but road rage seemed to agree with her.

'That's a cake,' she explained, calming down. 'I would offer you a piece, but I need all of it.'

I began to relax as I realised she really was driving me home, and wasn't planning to force-feed me the cake.

'You know, I'm the same sign as you,' she confided. I didn't know that, and I'm not pleased with the news. Like going to a party and bumping into a bitch with the same name and thinner legs. Or meeting someone from schooldays who's younger-looking than me.

'Fixed. Obsessional. Stubborn,' she said, tossing a smile in my direction.

The atmosphere took on that phony intimacy being alone in a confined space with a lunatic often provokes. The witch is stalking a man she had sex with eighteen years ago. His wife won't let him see her, but she knows he wants to. She drives to his house and waits outside in case he gets the chance to come out and fuck her. It turns out she needs the cake because *sometimes he doesn't come out until morning.*

Golly! Compared to her I'm normal. I know that when men go home at night and stay in until morning, it is not usually because their wives have tied them to the bed. What can you expect from a woman who works as a witch?

'Don't forget your magic,' she said, thrusting the potion into my hand as I left her truck forever. 'Be careful, there's enough in there to kill the street.'

The witch could be right. She could be wrong.

When Anna Kavan died there were 101 lipsticks

the same shade of pink in her bathroom and enough heroin to kill the street.

Kavan changed her name and her hair colour, but she never got over her addiction to pink.

It could be a magic potion.

I shake the small pink vial, listening for the swish. It could be lethal poison. One man's poison is another man's pleasure as Great-aunt Tatiana almost certainly didn't say.

And if I put a love potion in your drink when you're in love with me already, does it reverse the spell?

As an unfolding work-in-progress, anything can happen. Rape, murder, a happy ending? There's more than one escape route.

People may decide that Vivien Lash is twisted and not invite her to dinner parties. You may feel like your private conversations with her have been stolen and used as dialogue.

You may decide not to run away with her after all! Or you may be flattered to be part of the crazy cast, and decide to direct the movie.

Eating Custard with Stanley Kubrick

You invite me to lunch. You are interested in acquiring the movie rights to my *Creepy Neighbour* project. I pretend to believe you.

'It's called *Spying on Strange Men* now and stars me.'

'I bet it does.'

'But I'm not a man.'

'I'd noticed.'

Adding casually, 'See you both at lunch.' Now you have to bring your chaperone. You have to listen to me talk about art. You can't just go on about choices.

As you hang up, I pull petals off the yellow roses you sent me before going into your sulk.

You don't react when women die at your feet. You don't expect to be refused. Not by a woman with crazy ideas and no money. Someone who should admire your success, strive to share it, want to be you or want to fuck you like the new-fashioned movie star you are.

You are offended because you said I love you and I

didn't say it back.

We are in the Century Club, in the rooftop restaurant, sitting next to a big plant. Sometimes that's a bad idea. A wasp can suddenly fly out and sting you. Some people die from insect stings. Most people live.

'Normally he doesn't do lunch,' your assistant says, as we wait for your entrance.

'Neither do I,' I reply. 'I am usually asleep.'

She giggles, nervous. Sunlight is harsh on her orange hair. Has she really dyed her hair that colour? It seems so last century – something for Poles born under the sign of Pisces. Maybe it's for stubborn females who insist on making a stand against suburban blond but lack the nerve for sexy scarlet.

'He works very hard,' she says. 'He isn't one of those Soho people who sit around talking about it.'

You walk in and immediately a skinny woman with black hair rushes over and kisses you, just missing your mouth. I wonder if you've paid her. Not that you are undesirable. The timing is just too perfect.

I get the picture. You're admired, wearing a clean shirt, and have investors ready to finance the project. A new shirt, maybe? I'd be able to tell if I was close enough to smell the fabric. But you wouldn't risk wearing a new shirt for my benefit.

'We wondered which bits of *Spying on Strange Men* are 'real'?' the assistant asks, annoying me with her wiggling, phallic fingers.

You stare at me, eyes intense, while I answer. Your

eyes are not green after all. They are pale blue and threatening. My husband's eyes are green in the morning, before he drinks coffee, his gaze loitering between vulnerable and cruel.

The short answer is that it is all 'real'. It came out of my head. Everything in there is real. Even the things invented and imagined.

Your assistant, who is called Marion D Grottie, gets out her list and asks:

'One, did Creepy Neighbour rape you in real life?

'Two, does Creepy represent the dark side in all of us?' She looks at you when she says this.

'Or is he a political symbol, like the terrorist threat blighting our lives, the feeling that World War Three could start at any moment and make everything *meaningless*?'

She has clearly rehearsed these questions in advance to impress you. And you are playing her game: she looks like pigshit, she must be clever.

You watch me as I sip my water, leaving Grottie – can that really be her name? – to answer her own questions. She knows it's a trap but babbles on anyway, unable to avoid taking the bait.

We're not listening. At an inappropriate moment, you interrupt to tell me, 'In a long blonde wig and a chain mail dress, you could be a porn star.'

James says my voice is somewhere between porn and posh. You don't like hearing about him, but you can't stop asking about him.

'Are you mad or just playing?' Grottie asks, thrusting her notebook in between us.

'I like mad girls,' you say, switching off your phone as soon as it rings.

James says I'm frighteningly sane. He never ignores a ringing phone.

The story has changed since I whispered it in the dark. It's become more perverse, obsessive...twisted. Creepy Neighbour has his big purple gloves all over the plot.

Someone is going to be damaged, I don't know yet if it's me. I know it should be me - or there's really no risk at all. But maybe that spoils the fun. Perhaps it would be better if Creepy Neighbour tied James to a chair and stuck a banana in his mouth?

If you knew my husband, you would realise that's implausible.

Neither of us orders dessert, but we carry on talking, drinking black coffee, not smoking. I like the word desert, the way it means both sand and abandonment. Lonely stretches of parched sand.

I used to have silent dessert eating contests with Stanley Kubrick when I lived in his caravan. Who knows if he regretted his decision to let me eat in the commissary? You can't tell to look at me how much I can pack in.

Stanley's plate was overloaded with chocolate log, custard, cheesecake, crumble, any pudding going. Sugar is evil. But it depends on your attitude whether an addiction to cakes is humiliating.

Stanley, a naturally competitive man, was too dignified to acknowledge our contest out loud. Usually I won, but I cheated by not having a main course first.

I almost told you my Stanley story, but decided you might think I'm showing off. And these days I'm addicted to health. I don't look like an ex-sugar junkie.

Anyway, I don't talk about my past. It's a story full of preposterous coincidences and the shade of tall trees. Lies are easy to believe in but the truth sounds like something I've made up to amuse you.

I arrived in London penniless and found myself in Park Lane, opposite Hyde Park, as good a place as any to hide until morning. It's not the first time I've slept in a park. Not the first time I've run away.

I'd thought of switching to Holland Park, but that's a bit gay - too noisy at night. If I'd gone to Holland, I'd have missed the boy sleeping under the next bush. He introduced himself as Peter Pan but really he was Mad Jack, an extra in a Stanley Kubrick movie.

Stanley heard Mad Jack was sleeping in the park and invited him to live in his caravan, which was parked on the movie set. And the actor who was really an artist invited me.

Stanley's caravan was in Essex surrounded by palm trees. The trees cost $55 each and had been imported for his movie about the American war. He was never Stanley, he was always Mr Kubrick.

The caravan had no wheels, so we couldn't drive it somewhere else. It was parked on the black building set, by Beckton gas works, the derelict industrial estate that was now Vietnam. Because Mr K doesn't like flying, or driving faster than 35 miles per hour. If you crash at high speed your kidneys get mangled. Or he didn't fly, when he was alive. God knows what he's up to now.

Sometimes when asked why I have a photograph of myself with Stanley Kubrick on the wall of my kitchen, I pretend that the caravan was a trailer. Or people just assume I mean a trailer when I say caravan. Somewhere the star sleeps, showers, or has sex between scenes.

A trailer has a bathroom and a fridge full of champagne. The caravan wasn't plumbed, but we had access to the toilets in the commissary - deserted at night, apart from a security guard, who gave us a wide berth. He thought I was a very strange girl, and Mad Jack a far cry from sanity, and he was right. How can you be wrong about your opinions when they are subjective?

Later, when Stanley was dead and I had lost contact with everyone associated with that movie and the house in St Albans with no water in the fountain, I went to the real Vietnam and was mistaken for a Eurasian film star.

I can't say this out loud. I could, but I don't want to. You already resent me for being clever, I don't want to be interesting as well.

While we drink espressos and refine the plot, Marion

D Grottie sits watching. She doesn't drink coffee, it makes her 'go to the loo'.

'Surely you do that anyway?' I ask, making you laugh.

She excuses herself shortly after this remark, and you ask immediately.

'Remember the day we met?'

'No,' I lie.

You drum your fingers on the table, waiting for Grottie's return. This job is a temporary thing for her. She has a book in her along with her liver and kidneys. If our luck's in it will stay there. She has all the ambition of a plain woman gobbling a cheeseburger.

I want to confess that I do remember the day we met.

I was walking upstairs ahead of you. I could feel you behind me. I knew who you were, I'd seen you on TV. And I knew without turning round that you were The One. A glimpse at the door, the sensation of you watching me climb the stairs.

You asked to hire my jacket - a good opening line. Have you used it before?

'I need one just like it, for a film I'm making,' you said, a vulnerable boyish smile flickering at the edge of your composure.

You reached out to touch the white leather, and I stepped back, refusing your fingers.

'Is it fake?' you asked, embarrassed.

We are both people who resist being in love, who

deny the love object, who fear ruin. Dread exposure with a relentless intensity which makes natural breathing impossible. Understand that catastrophe and ecstasy go together like hate and love. How then could anything happen?

As usual you break the silence first.

'I'm getting married.'

I laugh out loud. 'You can't marry to spite me.'

Instead of issuing a denial, declaring love for your dimbo girlfriend, you smile casually and ask, 'Why not?'

Whispering, as the waiter brings us more water, 'A taste of your own medicine.'

When you lean closer, I can smell your new shirt.

I reach for your hand. You move away, start talking faster as you deliver your pitch.

'How many times have you been in love?' You sneak a glance at yourself in the mirror, and I know you've rehearsed this dialogue. I say nothing, forcing you to answer your own question.

'You only really love once.'

'What do you mean?'

'If you fall in love with a new person it means you never really loved the one you were married to.'

'A new love erases the old one?'

'Yes. If you run away with me you'll forget he ever existed.'

It's not possible to love two people at the same time. You always love one more than the other. The one you love most is the one you love.

I could have said nothing. But sometimes I can't resist showing off that I'm cleverer than you.

'The design is contaminated when you start to love the last person more than the next person.' The one you gave up but didn't get over. The one you left behind so that you could breathe again. 'That's why we need art,' I said.

'You've lost me.' Something I'm good at.

'It's a way of being seduced over and over without losing your purity.'

Love is the amateur's way of expressing art. But what is the artist's way of expressing love?

'The artist is the seducer as well as the seduced. Seduction is about risk. You have to risk something important. Flirting with Creepy Neighbour, Vivien Lash has to risk her own safety or it's...'

'But you're finished with that show...' You blurt this out, stop. Are you blushing?

My *Creepy Neighbour* show has sold out in advance of its opening next week. It's always the obvious stuff that sells.

'You're going to be a fucking star!' the gallerist told me.

I haven't told anyone. It's my secret, making me smile in my sleep. It occurs to me as I nurture my secret success that the anonymous collector could be you.

I carry on talking rubbish, concealing my emotions.

'If art is about risk, could something unspeakable be art. Something terrible but beautiful. Does evil have its own poetry?'

Hacking him to death with a meat cleaver. Making a pattern with the blood. You have to really love someone to kill them.

This is something I've been thinking about.

'You're talking in riddles to annoy me,' you say. 'But sooner or later you will have to make up your mind.'

The clock's ticking. We don't have all day. A cliché for every occasion.

'Life's too short,' you mutter, scowling.

When Grottie comes back from the 'loo', she senses instantly that you are sulking.

'It's fascinating to listen to your voice,' she says, working up to the insult rehearsed in the 'loo', where she has reapplied her thick make-up, which still doesn't cover up her acne. 'You have no accent…it's impossible to guess where you're from, or how old you are.'

I warm towards her pain, take pity on her. She loves you. It's hopeless. You're a man who takes beauty for granted. Demands extras on top. I'm your idea of original, superior to the fleshless bland beauties who kiss you every day. You imagine I'm unique.

Grottie is no one's idea of anything except maybe a dog crying in the dark. Her only hope is to have no hope. Declaring war with me of all people is absurd.

'Let's talk casting,' you say, switching your phone back on.

On the way home I realise that I know nothing about you. That's your appeal. There is nothing to know.

Your daydream hands touch me and the weight of your body crushes me, making escape possible in my imagination at least.

Dad is a good name for you because you're rich and good-looking and I want you to save me.

But it doesn't suit you. You're too young. Your heart hasn't been broken beyond repair yet. You need a name of your own. Something heroic, mysterious, perfect for a man with green eyes who lives in the present tense admired by the world.

My husband trusts me. He knows I will never leave him. His secrets are safe with me.

But it's too late for him. Too early for you. And where does that leave me? Alone in the bath with Deng Lijun singing about moonlight.

There are multiple ways of committing murder.

You can destroy the body. Or you can destroy the ability to dream. This mutilation of the soul is the most common form of self-murder.

My heart is separated from me. *He owns my heart*?

Is it love or stupid stubborn loyalty that binds me to him, traps me. Inability to abandon once I love. I can't leave him.

But I can kill him. Betrayal needs revenge. Lying is so suburban. Don't discard: destroy. A completion of symmetry.

I have a plot. A plan to execute. Something to be proud of. An accomplishment. A work of art.

I can't put it off until the next full moon. I can't wait until after my show, until I get rich, or any of my other excuses.

I am going to kill my husband as soon as he comes back. But when is he coming back? He never says. He just appears, sometimes in the morning as I'm waking up. Sometimes late at night as I'm falling asleep I hear his footsteps on the path.

I thought I heard him tonight. He paused by our palm trees, then walked on, stopping somewhere beyond my hearing.

I can't wait any longer. The bathwater is cold. I could phone you, make the first move for once, end the sulky silence.

You are not a replacement for him! He was a rehearsal for you.

And I'm getting better and better at breaking hearts without making myself cry.

I refuse to be a fucking victim.

Victims lack imagination. He spat on my heart, lied to me, and now he has to pay.

Love Will Tear Us Apart Again

It was easier, once I'd decided to kill him.

But I still have to be careful. One slip and I'm dead. It's him or me. So it has to be him.

I almost bumped into Creepy Neighbour on the garden path.

'It's a lovely night for a Cornetto,' he says.

Is he offering me an ice-cream, or just making an observation? Trying to sound interesting? Perhaps he has wind of my artwork? He looks impotent, not up to rape.

Ever since catching pneumonia on the night flight back from Havana, I haven't been hearing right. The other day I was asked outside a gym if I'd like to save two hundred pounds. I thought the woman was asking, 'Would you like to visit a gentleman's room?'

'Depends which gentleman,' I replied, confusing her.

Hearing is an important part of your equipment. But deafness has its advantages. Marilyn's pain can so easily become Marilyn melting in the rain.

Creepy Neighbour looks at me, soliciting a response. I smile without replying. I don't like fake Italian ice-cream anyway.

My white, clean home waits for me like heaven. Apart from the evil big bluebottle buzzing around, settling first on my white leather sofa, then on my marble dining table. How did this ugly thing even get in here?

I reach for the can of CS gas in my pocket, blinding myself without harming the giant fly. The Thing dances around me, gloating as I choke. Insects and humans have different nervous systems. Mr Novak, the paedophile teacher, taught us that.

'Be careful you don't choke to death,' Creepy says, when I run, coughing, into the garden. He's the kind of guy who could be damaged with a squirt of fly spray but his insides would be immune to anti-rape gas.

He leans against my palm tree, staring at my cleavage. To be fair, my chest is eye level for him. He'd have to stand on tiptoe to look me in the face.

'Nice night for it,' Creepy says, smirking.

For what? Raping your neighbour?

Familiarity is a false protection. Someone familiar, especially someone creepy, would not pick me as a target. Because everyone would *know* he did it.

Statistically I'm wrong. Most victims are murdered, raped and violated by people they know. Sometimes the murderer doesn't mind being caught. For Creepy Neighbour the game would be to kill the bitch from Number 13, have everyone in the building suspect, but get away with it.

No Raskolnikov confessions from Creepy. No guilt, no mistakes. My only defence is the can of Doom now in my bag to replace the CS gas squandered on the fly.

Also in my bag is a record of Creepy's activities. Elvis is still saving CCTV evidence for me. I didn't bother explaining that Creepy is no longer my installation. That show is dusted. I have the dress picked out already for my opening night.

Now I'm climbing the ladder to Hollywood, amazed by my overnight success. Who needs experience when you have ideas and a successful director on board? The Oscar's practically in the bag.

It's easier to take the evidence from Elvis and continue playing the Dicks Inc game until I leave town.

But the Creepy show bores me now. He goes in and out of his flat, carrying large bin bags. It may have been more interesting to conceal a camera in the bin room. Find out what he gets up to in there after dark. My nose draws the line at putting on a pair of rubber gloves and examining his rubbish.

My phone is ringing in my bag as I slam the door in Creepy's face and walk back into my own white heaven. The landline is ringing too; which one will I answer?

I don't look weak, indecisive. People say I have intelligent eyes. I appear to know what I am doing.

I stand staring at the phones, wondering which one is you and which one is him.

James could be calling to say when he's coming home. You could be calling to say you love me. First you have to know what you want, and then you have to take it.

I have to kill him when he gets home.

I'll write it down, make it real. But first I have to answer the phones. Or just leave them ringing?

It's you, all business, inviting me to discuss locations for *Spying on Strange Men*.

It's a business meeting, not a date. A lunch not a dinner. You have your pride. You're not going to throw yourself at me.

I'm half-listening to your voice as I tug at the wedding ring deforming my finger. It's easier to take off than put back on. Forcing it back on my finger, covering the bruise I made pulling it off. I don't want to send him a signal, give him a clue what I'm up to.

We make a date, or an appointment, depending on the mood. We need an end to our story. Or a beginning. The hate triangle in the middle is starting to bore me. Time's almost up. James is almost home.

I'm ready. And then the world blows up.

I Only Fall in Love with Strangers

The next day New York exploded and Ewan McGregor was sitting opposite me on the bus.

We are on the long seats, adjacent to the driver. He's wearing jeans and a fleece. I'm wearing my ironic white leather jacket, its lining marked with dust from Babylon.

I thought Babylon was a place invented by God, as a biblical parable, until I went there last year. Feet dusty from the streets of Cairo, a short metro ride away, because I couldn't stand the psycho taxis any longer. I lit a Coptic candle, received absolution from an armless ancient, bought a lapis lazuli bracelet, then caught the train back to Cairo and ate an omali for tea.

But names are seldom unique. There's more than one Babylon. There's more than one me. The Hanging Garden of Babylon was in Iraq, which used to be Mesopotamia, which sounds sexier. They don't sell bracelets in Eden these days.

These interior monologues are distracting me from the action. I don't want to think about bombs. I have a date with you tomorrow. I'd die rather than cancel, though my husband has called from Tel Aviv to warn me not to leave the house.

A lady with a fat nose is saying in a voice soaked in hysteria, 'People just get sick of being treated like shit!'

Her companion, a liberal looking male of indeterminate age dressed high street shabby, glances over his shoulder, embarrassed. The coarse woman has a point but nobody wants to hear it. Her comment focuses the mind on the Arab question, the inhumanity of arming their rich enemy.

And the hijackers have no demands! They don't want a fuel tank to South America or a delivery from McDonalds for their hungry hostages. They don't mind dying. That means they can't lose. My heart is beating fast with anxiety and awe when twenty Chinese people get on the bus.

A musical chairs style pantomime ensues. Ewan McGregor keeps smiling. He has a surprisingly nice smile for someone who's almost a movie star. The chief Chinese buys twenty tickets, one for everybody, then discovers he has only been given eighteen. Two of them are on the bus illegally.

Ewan's not my type. My type? Do I have a type?

The atmosphere in the bus is heightened. We're all in shock about the Twin Towers, but impersonating normality, taking the bus somewhere, being Green.

I am going to Marylebone to buy a pair of stiletto boots from Jesus Lopez. My husband has warned me not to go underground. UFO, our crumblie neighbour, thinks that James – who is always out of town - is responsible for the chaos.

'He's at it again,' she told me, as I passed her front door after seeing the explosion on News 24. UFO credits him with omnipotence.

'Wherever your hubby goes in the world, there's a revolution,' she said sweetly.

Everyone else is blaming Bin Laden. Except the Egyptian who said, 'Bin Laden could not have done this. Arabs are never on time!'

The woman behind Ewan McGregor is saying to her friend, 'I can't stay with him now. This sort of thing makes you think.' Her mind is focused on divorce, looking for excuses to confirm what she is thinking anyway. In a different mood, on a different day, the woman now focused on divorce could be using terrorism as an excuse to get married.

Being destroyed is better than being discarded.

Murder beats abandonment. Invisibility has always attracted him. Erasure not exposure.

Exciting and terrible at the same time, like falling in love with someone evil.

Great art has an unpredictable element. Some voyeurs love it, others hate it. Some see beauty. Others see doom. Some love or loathe the other characters in their world. Others feel nothing, allow nothing, as they drift through the drab movie of their life ignoring the plot twists and possibilities.

Some people are suspicious of truth, others of

invention. Danger and art belong together, inspiring and destroying each other.

Love always lies?

Now we've reached the pivotal moment in the movie when the hero's life has to change.

It's a matter of death and life. Wake up time. Time to separate the weak from the weak. That kill or be killed scenario. The fucker or the fucked.

One wrong turn and you're dead. It didn't occur to me you may be in danger; I was busy as usual thinking about me.

When I get off the bus God's tears stop and a rainbow appears, a magical arc in the sky, an escape route, a sign.

The first boots I try on are the right pair. The zip goes up without a hitch and I can walk without assistance. Ignoring the counter argument, I leave the shop wearing them.

When I go home there's a branch on my doorstep, hacked from one of our palm trees.

Maybe it just fell off? I don't want to turn into a paranoid loon. Not unless someone sends me a dead fish.

Double Indemnity is on. Barbara Stanwyck is almost beautiful. If she'd been more perfect she might have been less popular.

Elvis is obsessed with *Strangers on a Train*. He wants to swap murders with me. Criss-cross. But Elvis can't think of anyone he wants to kill. So I don't need to waste time explaining that we are not strangers, and not on a train.

My husband keeps phoning, he's worried about me, wants me to call off the Creepy project.

'Spying on your neighbour is a bad move,' he states the obvious. How can I tell him Creepy isn't taken seriously, he's just an extra in my story – not real at all, though he exists, waddling through the garden, fatter by the hour.

James wants me to give it up, find something else to amuse myself.

'Write a poetry collection,' he suggests.

The ladies at the High Commission come and go, fighting over Michelangelo.

I can't very well tell him Creepy was just a rehearsal for murdering him.

'Let's play *Double Indemnity*.'

'Yes,' you agree, surprised that I've phoned you instead of waiting for you give in and phone me. 'We'll kill your husband and live happily ever after.'

'He's not insured.'

'We'll do it for love.'

'They get caught.'

'Only because they betray each other.'

'Is there a movie about murder with a happy ending?'

'Yes.'

'I can't think of one.'

'*Spying on Strange Men.*'

The doorbell rings. I put down the phone, but don't hang up.

The cream envelope is propped against one of our palm trees. The one James says is me, the smallest one. The tall one is him, standing guard over me.

I don't have to open the envelope.

I don't want to see. But I do. It will make me hate him again. Fresh hate will help me.

The same thick expensive creamy paper as before, the cloying scent of the glue.

The face in the picture gives me a fright.

The identity of the woman isn't in doubt this time. But where was the picture taken? And why are you sending it to me?

Say Hello, Kiss Goodbye

This time we meet alone. To discuss our movie, plan our escape.

Together in the crowd, ordering the same extra dry vodka martini. Stirred not shaken with a lime twist. The barman doesn't even need to look at the vermouth, just have it in the room.

Your flat joke lolls in the air between our mouths, not bothering anyone. You don't usually drink during the day. Not reckless enough to get drunk and do your job at the same time.

I'm taking a risk, about to tell you The Truth. After all we could be blown up any minute.

Before I say anything, you get in first as usual, making make me an offer I shouldn't refuse.

You write down an amount.

'Is that what I'm worth?'

You double it, showing off.

'Yours to do what you like with.'

You pick up my hand, abandoned palm down on the table. Today your fingers feel cold. When I pull away the diamonds in my eternity ring scratch you.

What I *like*?

'So you don't need him. You can choose.'

You wouldn't be buying me, you'd be making a gift of freedom. As long as I choose you.

You breathe out and suddenly I'm aware I'm holding my breath, still waiting for a sign. Or maybe it's a shove I need in the wrong direction so that all the wrong turns become obvious under the cruel glare of street lights and the signs are at last easy to read.

'But you're too late. I have money of my own.' I watch your face for a reaction. 'My show's sold out already.'

But you know that, don't you? You are Mr Mystery, the anonymous collector. Your gesture lies somewhere between touching and annoying.

You want to save me. You want to control me? Maybe you just like my work.

It's not that much. It won't last a lifetime.

The voice of doubt whispers even when the sun shines.

Nothing lasts forever. Why would I even want it to?

'It's totally obvious you're going to be a star,' you say, staring at my white feet. I've kicked off my shoes, but I'm not massaging your thigh with my bare foot. After all, we're not in Italy.

Today my toes are dipped in blood, a similar shade to the Choosy Cherry of my childhood.

Ritual breaks infinity into small boring steps. When I was 14 I thought I was old, running out of time. I had to escape, to run away from home before getting trapped by poverty and fear.

Your eyes are on my feet, seeking the scar which stopped me dancing. That doesn't feel like a death sentence anymore. The diseased bone was bad luck not divine judgement.

You make a confession. You had cancer last year. You're not perfect after all. You lost your hair. It grew back. A lie to give us sickness in common? Not a sexy lie. Maybe it's true. Maybe I don't care.

'A bum is an inverted heart,' the girl behind us says, American accent contrasting the strange observation.

You look at me, eyebrow slightly raised.

Suddenly, in the middle of laughter, I become aware of someone watching me. Glancing up, I realise Olga Borga is our waitress. She half smiles, stops when I don't respond. Making her face blank, she deposits our drinks and disappears behind the bar.

Small acts of sadism keep my hand in. It would have been easy to say hello, ease her embarrassment. The snub has made her feel worthless. But if I allow my mask to slip, my kind heart to show, I'd start to feel her pain. Everyone's pain would swallow me. I can't live in a vomit of empathy. I have my own problems!

Of course it's not Olga Borga, just a woman who could be cast as her in a movie - if she was an actress, and Olga Borga ever merited a biopic.

The double, the other, the evil twin is always lurking in the mirror.

Something I've been thinking about, suddenly you say it out loud.

'I wish I'd been in New York, I'd love to take photographs. There's something beautiful about it.'

You mean the WOW factor which was edited out of the news. The voyeur who said, 'Wow,' when the second tower was hit was responding to a scene from a movie or computer game, even though it's happening in real life on a misty New York morning.

'Ultraviolence as Art,' you say, ruining the mood. You're at it again, trying to impress me with your big brain.

You leave me alone, go to talk to somebody important.

You keep looking over at me, making sure I still exist. I couldn't stop thinking about Olga Borga's four-leaf clover.

Darko told her to make a wish when she found the four-leaf clover at the school picnic. Olga Borga wished for sacks of gold and diamonds.

'That's a stupid wish,' I said, taking the clover from her. 'I wish for all the power in the world,' I said, smiling at Olga Borga for Darko's benefit, 'so I can take all your gold from you.'

'How clever,' the sewing teacher said to Darko, 'she thinks in concepts.'

'Who would you be?' she asked me, 'if you had all the power in the world?'

I said my name.

'Who else?' she persisted, wanting me to say God.

So I didn't.

'Me the Omnipotent,' I said.

Everybody laughed and we all enjoyed the picnic except Olga Borga who never enjoyed anything. Was Darko buggering her then? Or was that something she had to look forward to?

There are glamorous victims and victims. Did Olga Borga convert herself with nicotine, material success, and surprisingly long eyelashes into a glamorous victim? A subject for fantasy on a rainy afternoon, but not a life's work.

Olga Borga was not raped, she was abused. Labels are important. Rape implies illicit pleasure even if it isn't yours. Abuse makes you a victim. A victim grants permission.

'What you thinking about?' you ask, interrupting my gloom.

'Charlotte Rampling.'

'Why?'

'She was born to have headaches.' You laugh. You don't need a debate. James would have touched my head, force-fed me a painkiller, maybe called the doctor for some opium tabs just in case. You never know how a headache will develop.

'I like mad girls.'

'My husband says I'm frighteningly sane.'

'Maybe he doesn't know you as well as he thinks.'

'When did you take those pictures?'

'What pictures?'

'The ones you left on my doorstep.'

'I've never been to your place.'

'Right.'
'Except to spy on you.'

After a latte, which you apologise for drinking, you suddenly become less serious, more flirtatious with an element of sexual threat in your pale blue eyes.

Grottie joins us, to take notes, and you order a glass of Chablis to cover the anti-social stench of milk, and let it slip that you haven't read my new draft of the *Strange Men* script.

'I do all his reading for him,' Grottie says triumphantly.

Intended as an insult, it pleases me. Confirms the obvious: you're in love with me.

I tell you about this story. You're a character in it. It's my love letter to you.

'What story?'

'My diary – the book that goes with the *Strange Men* movie.'

You laugh, delighted, asking if I've used your real name?

There it is. I've said it. Told you The Truth. Admitted out loud that I love you, with a witness present. You are of course none the wiser because of my cryptic storytelling technique. You can tell I'm flirting with you, but don't know whether or not it's real. Any minute I could flash my wedding ring in your face.

Grottie watches us, sulking. She doesn't see the point of this. We're all going to die anyway. She's eaten a bread roll, living dangerously – ignoring her allergies.

As we laugh, lean closer together, suddenly she interrupts, affronted by our happiness. 'New York's just been blown up!'

And you reply, 'Art becomes more important in war.' Trying to impress me again. He doesn't have to try.

'Your face has changed,' you say as we stand in sunlight saying goodbye.

'It's different every time I see you.'

My face is reflected in the window of a Chinese shop selling hair accessories and sandalwood soap. It looks the same to me.

Maybe my face is the same. Could that be the trick? You are seeing me in a different light.

You lean forward to kiss my cheek but I don't do social kissing. I only kiss men that I fancy. At the last minute, as your lips are about to make contact with my skin, I turn suddenly. Forcing you to kiss my mouth.

You lean in closer and this time I don't move. I think about nothing. Light and empty and clean. Our first kiss has the intensity of a last kiss. I feel happiness reaching out to me and this time I'm not pushing it away.

'I didn't leave any pictures on your doorstep.'

'You just like to spy on me.'

'Every night.'

James is coming home for my opening night party on Thursday. I'll murder him afterwards. It's a deadline. A ticking clock. Something to help me focus.

And after I kill him we can escape.

I don't know that it's too late already. The goalposts have been shifted again and worse than that they are invisible to my naked eye.

I'm Your Man

Creepy is asleep in his MG, parked by Camera One on the forecourt of the building, when I get home.

Is he guarding his parking space? Or hoping to trap the person who left the bum imprint on his bonnet?

He suspects me of tampering with his precious old car. Nothing has been said out loud but he makes accusations with his bloodshot eyes, sizing up my bum with bulging interest.

He's plotting a move, getting ready to pounce, and I've used all my CS gas on a big fly.

Passing through the garden, I take a look in Creepy's window at the familiar anal pink upholstery. No sign of anyone inside. He's snoozing in the car park, and Mrs Creepy must be at work.

'Her husband died then Creepy moved in with unseemly haste,' UFO told me. 'There is no truth in the rumour that I'm giving the handyman handjobs behind the bins,' she insisted, with strict and detailed instructions to repeat this information to no one. Though it is not necessary for me to repeat it because she has told everyone already.

'Why is she called UFO anyway?' James asked, before going off to save the world.

'She saw one land in the garden last time there was a full moon.' And it's a good name for her. When I'm exasperated I can shout, 'U FO.'

Why be polite to someone nosy and vulgar just because they are decrepit? Well, appearances are important and we are all respectable people here.

'There are no rats, Presbyterians or anyone who shops at Harrods living in this building,' UFO told me, soon after we moved in.

The synagogue next door now has a guard at its entrance, hoping to head off the Arab trap. I can see his flashlight flickering in and out of view between the bushes as I close the midnight blue velvet bedroom curtains.

James phones to say Goodnight. I run to the phone, thinking it's you, almost knocking over the photograph on the dressing-table.

What would happen if I smashed it? Would that be a signal, a sign, a bad omen? Or a relief, something to cleanse the young me who's now the old me, leaving me to resurrect and start again?

'You're out of breath,' James says, suspicious, when I pick up the phone.

He asks me to look for his watch. Maybe it's in his bathroom. No.

'Aren't you wearing it?'

'I left it behind,' he laughs, 'to keep an eye on you.'

It's a proper spy watch with a camera and

microphone concealed inside.

'It's not here.'

'Have another look,' he says, 'and call me back if you find it.'

What's he up to? James never loses anything.

Is there something in his bathroom he wants me to find? Evidence of fidelity maybe, hidden under the bottle of perfume from Babylon? Is it even called perfume when it's worn by a man?

I'm always losing things. Nothing's ever where it's supposed to be including my thoughts.

What am I looking for now?

Nothing. I've found you. Somebody to drive the getaway car.

I've always disliked people who want to find themselves. It's much better to lose yourself and steal someone else's soul. Or borrow it, and give it back later, once you've sucked out the interesting bits.

I'm bored, nervous, excited. A feeling something is about to happen, a tension in the moonlight.

Two days left until my show opens. Two days until James comes home.

I unbolt the door, stand in the garden for a few minutes breathing in. The scent of jasmine and honeysuckle makes me imagine I'm not in England.

Someone has stubbed out a cigarette in my palm tree. I remove it, check for lipstick stains, then throw it at Creepy Neighbour's door.

I go back in, switch on the television; press play. I may as well watch the Creepy show one last time. The repetition of him plodding past the cameras may send me to sleep.

Creepy creates a shadow on my window on his way to the bins.

It's midnight. I'm sitting on the floor in candle-light, sipping Nuits St Georges, daring it to spill on the white carpet. The Creepy show's playing silently; my television reflected into the garden making two of him as he appears in real time.

09.11 Creepy passes Camera Two carrying dry cleaning. He walks like a woman.

14.42 Creepy comes umbrella first through the gate, pointing it at me like a musket.

16.02 Creepy is talking to UFO outside his bed-room window. She enquires about his wife and Creepy replies, 'She is on an extended holiday with her mother.'

UFO reported this dialogue to Elvis, and for once the lip sync matches her memory of the conversation.

'She hasn't sent me a postcard either,' UFO said.

'Does she usually send you postcards?'

'Oh yes, I save the stamps for my cat.' That may be true and it may not be. Her cat's a queer cunt who could have a stamp album in its faux mink basket.

Creepy doesn't return from the bins. At least, I don't see his shadow crossing my window.

There's something wrong. I'm not sure what. I re-wind and watch again, while we talk on the phone.

'I saw you coming towards me at the airport, on one of those moving runways. You were going somewhere. I was going home. You didn't see me. As my runway passed yours, I almost called out your name. But you looked like someone else.'

I'm about to say you have it wrong, it must really have been someone else, because I haven't been to the airport this week. When I realise you're describing a scene from a movie.

'Let's run away straight after your show,' you say suddenly. You make it sound like a joke, in case I don't like the idea.

'Yes,' I agree immediately.

Instead of acting out the ritual until the end, we just leave it out in the rain to drown while we live happily ever after. We're not like other people after all.

'Let's go now. Tonight!' I say, surprising you.

But you can't go tonight. You have to finish shooting a commercial or no one will ever insure you again.

'It's just two days,' you say, 'we can leave straight after your party.'

'No we'll go before that. As soon as you finish shooting on Thursday...It's best to leave before he gets home,' I say, immediately regretting the use of that word.

There is no escape from home. The husband must die before we disappear into The End. Otherwise he will follow.

He will always bring me home. Force me to come back to him. Make me sorry. Punish me for loving him again and again and again.

Unless…what if, like Elvis, I'm dead already? No one can see him hiding behind the net curtain at Gracelands, except the other Elvis. What if I become invisible to everyone except myself?

You'll never get a glimpse of God until you stop looking.

'It's kind of cool, missing your opening night party,' you say. 'Like Garbo.'

Being mysterious could make my work more valuable. That, and dying.

You have to get up early but I keep you talking. I want to listen to your voice until one of us falls asleep. Listening to you breathe makes me feel safe.

'*Double Indemnity*,' you say.

'Is that the new password?'

'Yes.'

But you're wrong. Insurance is immoral. The policies are rigged so that only the company benefits. The real password, the one more important than love or even escape, is freedom.

My freedom was contaminated when I tried to take out an emotional insurance policy to protect me from love. Instinctively I know this but it doesn't harden into consciousness until it's too late.

'I have to go to sleep now,' you say.

'No…don't go.'

'We'll be together forever soon.'

Forever. That word gives me the creeps, hanging

in the distance between us like a warning I will never see you again.

'Every time you leave me for a minute it feels like goodbye.'

But you don't hear me. You're asleep already. That's James' line anyway.

After hanging up, I check to make sure the front door is bolted and go to bed. Lights out. Darkness. The scent of jasmine from the garden.

Lights on. Look under the bed. Nobody home. That word again, following me, mocking. Is home the place of birth, the place of happiness, or where you live? A place of safety, a place of suffocation. A cocoon, a tomb.

When talking on the telephone, you can tell if the other person isn't listening even when there's no background fidget soundtrack.

Falling asleep I know you are dreaming about me even though there is no evidence. I can smell your cigarette burning down in the dark, the one you almost finished smoking. I believe that you love me.

I've missed the deadline for dying young but it's never too late to escape.

Elvis is in the Boiler Room

Mrs Creepy is really missing. She's not in the movie anymore. She's on holiday with her mother, allegedly; but Elvis didn't see her leave for the airport.

And Mrs Creepy doesn't even have a mother, according to UFO, though Elvis begs to differ.

'Everybody has a mother even if it's a stork,' he told me, sure of himself.

Elvis is disgusted by UFO trying to muscle in on our meetings. Her knickers have gone missing and the fire brigade and police are not taking it seriously. Now she has come to us for help.

We are running a serious murder investigation and this old bean is making a mockery of our detective work. But it's a communal garden. We can't ask her to leave.

'We could kill her,' Elvis suggests. Murder is contagious. Once it's in the air, everyone catches the bug, fantasising about eliminating enemies. 'Tick tock, tick tock,' he says.

'You mean criss-cross?'

'Noughts and crosses?'

'*Strangers on a Train.*'

'Elvis loves trains! Did I tell you about the time...'

'Yes.'

'I can't keep up, Miss.' Elvis looks troubled. 'Elvis is slow today.'

He's slow every day, but I don't want to make him cry again, like he did when I told him I've changed my mind about being his partner in detecting crime.

I had to make light of it, pretend it was a joke, to stop snot drizzling from his long nose to his pumped up Elvis pout.

'How would we dispose of the body?'

'What body?'

'UFO's.'

'Is she dead?!'

'She will be when we murder her.'

'Oh, Elvis gets it...' He taps his nose. 'We shouldn't really be talking about this here.' He pokes a bush with a stick. There's nobody hiding in there.

'We need to go down below.' He points at the grass, meaning the boiler room, which to be fair is almost directly under where we're standing.

He leans in close and whispers, 'We could leave her lying on the path with her panties covering her eyes. People would think she died of natural causes on account of her being addicted to Harvey's Bristol Cream.'

Not with her pants on her face they won't. But I don't mention this on account of not believing that a murder will ever take place in this garden.

Instead of killing our mad neighbour, we make a date to meet in the boiler room, one that I'm not planning to keep.

There's no time left to waste. Not with Bin Laden up to his tricks and James coming back any minute to celebrate my *Creepy Neighbour* opening night party. My first solo show in a gallery but I don't need to worry about what to wear because I won't be there.

Elvis has registered our business, Dicks Inc, and has everything insured up to the eyeballs. But I'm just acting casual, carrying on as normal, whatever the fuck that is, until we escape tomorrow.

The plot thickens.

Elvis comes to tell me that Creepy has left his spare keys at reception for the *gas man*. This is a source of Hitchcockian suspense, because there is no gas in the building apart from the boiler in the basement.

I should tell him I'm busy and shut the door in his face. But he's standing there in his red sparkly jump-suit, full of glee at this new clue, and I don't want to crush his spirit.

Elvis is all for creeping into Creepy's flat on the spot to look for clues. Crouching outside his bedroom window, we could hear him snoring. But I smell a trap. Creepy is the kind of dude who would record himself snoring in order to fool snoops into thinking he's asleep.

The gas man is a ruse to lure us in there. And he's

waiting behind the bedroom door with a hatchet.

I sent Elvis to the Magic Cobbler to have the keys copied, then he returned the original set to Creepy saying, with a straight face, 'The gas man's been already.'

Creepy put the keys in his waistcoat pocket with a sinister smile – according to Elvis, who is prone to exaggeration.

'The keys to his lair are safe and sound in your palm tree, Miss,' Elvis says.

And they can stay in there with the worms. Creepy is giving me the creeps. Two cockroach eyes are on me every time I pass his door. I can feel him standing behind the peephole, examining the distorted piece of me he can see.

'Elvis will be back when darkness falls...The password tonight is *Love Me Tender*.'

Did Creepy really murder his wife? Is that why he's always taking large black bags to the bins?

I can't help thinking, even though I know it isn't nice, that would be great publicity for my show.

Symmetry attracts the eye. I want a tidy end to this story, before we start our new story.

But real life is untidy. My husband's right. Pushing Creepy over the edge is a bad move. Rape isn't art. It's too real. I'm a nosyparker, not an idiot. Joyce Grenfell's on my mind, the papers are full of her.

Joyce Grenfell was a lady psychiatrist in the Scrubs who gave the murderers – including Elvis's mate – electric shocks on their penises for their *own good*. Why can't people admit they are just making their own fun? Instead of these phony excuses and half-baked explanations.

The sadistic psychiatrist reminded me of Joyce Grenfell, the actress from the St Trinian's movies, who people claim was attractive in real life. To look at the shrink, staring out from the front page of *The Standard*, you wouldn't believe she'd go anywhere near a luststick let alone with an electric prod.

But she tempted fate too far. There were too many men with burn marks on their bits and *Panorama* got wind of it. Joyce took early retirement. She was living in Ealing or Borehamwood, someplace with an old studio, when one of her victims tracked her down and hid in her wardrobe until it was time to give her a taste of her own medicine.

Creepy doesn't need to track me down, I'm already here.

Elvis will have to go into number four tonight and hide under the bed alone.

I've retired from the Dick business. Murder is one way to escape but it isn't mine. I've been invisible before. A new name, a new hair colour, a new me. My happy ending.

And there's a pile of silk knickers on my bed – the ones you bought me in Hong Kong – waiting to be packed. The white leather suitcase is sitting patiently on the floor.

My hands are shaking. How many pairs of shoes do I need? You will buy me new ones.

Do I need to take anything?

My diary. That's mine. Best to burn it or bury it in the garden instead of taking it with me?

The jewellery is all from James. The ruby choker from Jaipur that the maid assumes is fake because I leave it lying casually on my dressing-table. The blue diamond ear-rings I never take off even when I'm asleep. The black pearls I can't leave behind. But if I take them with me they will forever remind me of him.

I'm spying on myself in the mirror, staring at the pearls when I notice it's missing.

The picture of me, the young perfect one he married, isn't sitting on top of the glass dressing-table. Did I move it when I was fed-up being watched? I know that I didn't.

Has James taken it with him? Why would he do that? The gap in the dust betrays where the picture was before. It must have been sitting there last time the lazy maid polished the glass. I told her not to come this week. She works for James, not me. She's his creature.

She could have stolen the photograph? Why would she do that?

Maybe I put it in the suitcase already? But there's nothing in there except an ankle chain you bought me in Havana, for a laugh, ha ha ha.

Then I remembered the spare keys at reception for

the cleaner or the gas man, whoever needs to come in while I'm out.

Nobody can get in when I'm home. The door is bolted from inside. The windows are locked.

As a precaution, I may as well collect the keys.

Elvis had left the building.

'He doesn't work here anymore,' Miguel says. 'Miguel is doing a double shift, Madam.'

Why does everyone around here refer to themselves in the third person?

I can talk, calling myself Vivien Lash! You have a new name for me already. You're going to tell me tomorrow when we meet at the airport. One story ends, a new one begins. You haven't told me yet where we're going.

'It's a surprise,' you said, but I know you are taking me back to Havana, even though that's the first place he'll look. We can change the tickets. You can do anything when you're rich.

That isn't true. It's a fantasy. But it's a convincing fantasy.

My spare keys are not in the safe.

'Your husband has them,' Miguel grins. 'He took them last time.'

'Last time?'

'Yes,' Miguel smiles, pleased we agree.

There's no point arguing with a man who doesn't

speak your language.

Nobody can get in when I'm asleep, even with keys, but I wish you weren't working late. I wish we could go now.

I don't want to make a fool of myself calling you and crying. I should have done. I may have saved both of us.

Creepy looks smug when I pass his door on my way back through the garden.

He's sitting outside in an Edwardian chair, wearing his smoothie outfit, eating a vaginal cream puff with jam oozing down his chin. I could never love a man who eats sugar.

His keys are still where Elvis hid them in the palm tree by my front door. Does Creepy have my spare set? It doesn't matter. I'll be gone by tomorrow. I'll keep the door bolted until then. I'm safe. Home free.

If I keep telling myself that, I'll start to believe it. And then it will come true.

Raising a glass of red wine to his wet lips, Creepy says something to me.

I can't make out what he's saying - because my deaf ear's turned in his direction - but I know he's really saying, *Come on, cunt.*

Well, the creep isn't going to goad me into going in there in search of Mrs Creepy. I didn't like her hair anyway. What do I care if she's been dismembered? That's her hard cheese for taking up with Creepy in the first place. For all I know she could be in

Barbados with her crumblie mum, sipping rum punch and fantasising about black men.

Then I discovered my knickers were missing.

Distracted by my palm trees at the front door; a bum had clearly sat on one of them, leaving a sample of pubic hair on one of its fronds. How could I have failed to notice on my way out?

Ringing phone interrupts my inspection. I run to answer, hoping it's you.

My husband's calling, I can hardly hear. His voice almost drowned out not by background noise but interference on the line. He sounds really far away.

He won't be back tomorrow after all. A woman in his field trip was eaten by a lion yesterday. She went on safari for some r&r and this lion had her for breakfast.

He is going to be delayed attending her funeral and dealing with the report she didn't finish. The agenda changes from hour to hour. He's out meeting destiny instead of waiting for shit to happen.

'Sorry, Baby, I'm going to miss your show.'

I'm not his baby. That's a name for the silly sluts he stooped to, living down to their expectations with cheap lies.

'Send me some pictures, so that I can see you in your new dress.' But I can't because I'm missing my show too. I have more exciting plans.

'What colour's your dress again?' The scarlet dress I'm wearing to leave him.

The African night is under curfew so he can't talk long. He has to drive back to his hotel before dark because it's not safe to stop at red lights - those men with long knives jump into the car and decapitate anyone white with a wallet.

The phone went dead as we were talking. I assumed the problem was at his end.

What's he up to? Is he with some girl with a big bum and home-dyed hair who feels important with a foreign man? Makes him feel powerful – kissing her engorged mouth, looking down on her cheap clothes; excited by his own superiority. She pretends to be a virgin, he pretends to be rich. Mutual distrust the basis of attraction; they despise each other.

I don't need to waste any more time wishing the past could be erased.

Nothing will ever be the same again. This terrifies and excites me.

I pour a glass of vodka, forget to sip it, start running my bath, the sound of clean water cheers me up. The jar of rose petals is empty but I don't need them. I have the jasmine and sandalwood oil you had mixed for me in Damascus.

Then I noticed my knickers were missing.

All of them. It's implausible. They were on the bed a minute ago. Unless I put them in the suitcase already? Filling a bag is a reflex action.

I open it and take a look, knowing they will not be inside.

Has UFO buried them in the garden to authenticate the theft of her discoloured M&S drawers? Maybe there's an underwear thief on the loose? It could be the squirrel addicted to cashews who lives in the bougainvillea. Or the cat who rapes with his paw?

I lie on my bed, face squashed into the pillow.

I lack the commitment to be addicted to anything, according to you. But do you really know me? And does that even matter. The philophobic's cut isn't the deepest? If I escape, will I be able to breathe?

As I'm running to check that the door is bolted, a text message from a number I don't recognise appears on my phone.

HELP

My bath's still running. Switch it off. No. Step into it. It will calm me down.

A gulp of vodka, it tastes funny. The skanky cleaner hasn't rinsed the glasses right; leaving a bitter aftertaste in my mouth.

The bath doesn't help. The scarlet bath. Scarlet on the white. When they cut you open to find out how you've been murdered your insides will be perfect silent red.

You never really see yourself, the image reverses in the mirror. But it all comes right in the end, in a photograph, so long as the lighting tricks the eye to see perfection.

What the fuck am I talking about? I'm stalling. Pretending nothing's wrong. Any minute he'll come in with a hatchet and chop me up into little pieces. Or big bits. It's supposed to happen in the shower but who says it can't be the bath? There are no guarantees. Nothing's sacred including a sacrament.

I always fall in love with strangers. Eating cake in Damascus maybe, thinking of you.

When I went back into my bedroom, the first thing I noticed was the pair of scarlet silk knickers sitting on the pillow waiting for me.

There is no blueprint for this moment. No rehearsal. Your voice would only make me cry now. I'd start to doubt. Imagining I'm not allowed to replace him with you. Deep down I don't believe it's possible to escape even when I've done it again and again and again.

My phone rings as I reach for the can of Doom in my bag.

Before answering, I look behind me to make sure I'm not in a *Dial M for Murder* moment.

'Hello,' a woman's voice says, 'It's...'

'Wrong number,' I reply, terminating. It isn't the time to argue with a suspicious woman, I have a pair of red pants sitting on my pillow watching me. Maybe there's a note underneath?

No. The gesture is just a warning.

I can come into your flat and sniff your underwear any time, cunt.

The phone rings, her again.

'I am calling about...' She says your name. It sounds better when you say it. 'He's...' she says.

He's dead? My ears are playing tricks on me again. She can't really have said that?

'A terrible accident...I thought you'd like to know.' This time she terminates.

I call and call but you don't answer. My phone rings. It's you!

But it's not you. It's Marion D Grottie using your phone. She babbles on. I'm trying to listen, but I can't hear her.

'It's upsetting for me to say this,' Marion D Grottie says, 'but he loved you, really loved you. It wasn't a game.' She can't resist adding, 'Not for him.'

'I don't believe you!'

'I am telling the truth,' she says. 'Why would I lie?'

'He's waiting for me at the airport.'

'You're hysterical.'

'You evil lying bitch!'

'I am hanging up if you continue to abuse me. I called you out of kindness.'

'Kindness! You're pretending he's dead out of kindness!'

'He's been *run over by a train*. Believe me or not. It will be in the paper soon enough.'

Things like that don't happen in real life. Men don't get run over by trains. Your head, separated from your body, is rolling away from the track. Another memory of a sight I haven't witnessed.

'Are you still there?' her voice asks. But I've dropped the phone.

Picking up the red pants to check if they are wet with water or blood; I raise them to my nose, then run to be sick. The toilet lid is down. Sense of dread when I lift it.

An evil big shit stares up at me. Someone has made a massive brown mess and not flushed. It wasn't me, I haven't eaten all week. The brown stuff isn't something I'd forget doing. Or leave dissolving in the dark.

And what does the D stand for? Marion Dobermann Grottie? These thoughts fly through my mind as I wonder what the fuck to do?

The last thing I remember is the smell. The smell of the sea, the pure clear green sea of my childhood coming up to meet my nostrils; knocking me out.

Killer's Kiss

I woke in the boiler room, lying naked on the concrete floor, tied with a chain.

I'm not cold, just tired, with a dry tongue. The red pants fill my mouth, silencing me. A cockroach makes its way to the light, I watch its advance, holding my breath.

Rats are admired in China. Intelligent, adaptive, almost immortal. But nobody loves a cockroach for obvious reasons.

With surprise, I realise I am in my bed at home, asleep. Having one of those dreams where I am awake. But only awake in the dream. In real life, I'm still asleep.

It made sense at the time.

Looming over the bed, looking at me, holding his breath.

Something is about to happen. A decisive atmosphere hangs between us, ripe with irretrievable potential.

You think you're dreaming, but this is real.

There is no more dialogue. I wait for him to say something. Form words in my own head, don't say them out loud.

What does everything mean?

What does anything mean?

Suddenly I am on the floor, the white carpet prickling my flesh vaguely scented with Moroccan rose. Picked in moonlight by happy people. Nothing must contaminate the purity of the petal. Evil memories hide everywhere. Until you can imagine it, it isn't real.

The windows are closed. No fragrant breeze drifts in from our garden. We always sleep with them open. His body pushes against me then changes its mind, takes me to the black marble dining table.

A better view from here, a drawer full of knives. The Chinese chopper, the African dagger.

Bury your past in a successful future.

Battering me hard, avoiding my face, seeking a reaction. Each time just missing my flesh, hitting the table.

Cruelty is a sign of love.

Blood always feels like water. The smell familiar, the texture tricking me again.

How did you get in here?

I used my key.

A surprised voice as if this is natural behaviour I am absurd to question. The door was bolted from the inside.

That can't keep me out.

He was inside already, spying on me, waiting to pounce, to punish me for spitting on his heart. He's been watching me all along.

My white leather suitcase sits on the floor ready to escape.

Packed full of my favourite things, heavy. I should have known. Never wait until morning. Get out while the going isn't good. You told me so. You warned me.

It's too late!

Now I'm in his power. He has a night to linger over revenge and a morning to avoid repercussions before you start to miss me.

I've cried wolf so many times, when I don't turn up at the airport you will probably curse me and take the flight alone. Not worry about me at all as you drink vodka martinis in neon moonlight, let alone rush to my rescue.

But you're dead. That was just a nightmare? Your girlfriend didn't phone. Marion D Grottie was playing tricks on me. Suzy Leather wasn't eaten by a lion. Men don't get decapitated by trains, not in England.

'It's all a mistake,' my husband's voice says, and I can hear the black pearls falling one by one to the floor. I wouldn't be seen dead in pink or white.

'Everything's ruined.' Did I say that, or was it him;

or even you?

Someone is knocking on the door. It's you, come to save me at last! But it's Creepy Neighbour complaining about the noise.

As I hear the door close and his footsteps recede along the garden path, I notice our new wallpaper.

It's my face, blown up poster sized, duplicated over the walls. The back of your head's in the shot. Or is it James?

The next picture shows us in profile kissing in the street. Our first kiss was our last.

It wasn't you?

If you didn't send me the pictures, who left them on my doorstep?

First the whore; then the wife. It's the obvious questions that confuse until the answer is staring you in the face along with oblivion.

There is only one person it could have been. A punishment? A test?

He's the one. The only one forever; watching over me.

And it's impossible after all to control your destiny, fix your life, escape your self, rewrite the end.

Except in your head. Except he is in my head too. The trick is to remember that I'm in his heart. He can punish me, but I can hurt him. I can make his soul bleed. It is a small consolation.

Loneliness is almost the same word as loveliness.

I manage to say this out loud. He hears me. The escape money's in my account already. Safe. Waiting. Expanding.

No strings?

If I start believing you, I'll know that this party fears two.

Violence in the air finds its friends.

A suicide bomber, a brisk slap on the face, an explosion to shake the world then in turn be forgotten like Flash Gordon's troubles in Krypton. Serenity descends after the storm, the birds sing, and we're happy.

No, no. That's wrong. Flash Gordon is from a galaxy far far away? Superman is from Krypton, and look where flying around in a fag outfit landed him. Paraplegics are at the front of the queue for the toilet.

I don't have a thing to worry about. That's the beauty of pain. It's a relief. Now I'm safe from choice. He has chosen for me. You hesitated and lost, afraid of appearing foolish. Now you're stopped dead in your tracks, eating custard with Stanley Kubrick on a fluffy black cloud.

Relief covers me with myself. I stroke his face, touching his tears. Buried against my heartbeat, I feel him smile when I promise never to leave him. I don't *want* to leave him. Escape is easy if it coincides with desire.

I'm yours forever.

I know.

Fear and Desire. Killer's Kiss. Naked Kiss. No that was someone else's movie. And *Fear of Love* isn't a movie at all, it's ugly and ordinary like the common cold.

Memories live in a room awaiting recognition. I don't want to forget. Happiness would be destroyed as well as lies. Sometimes fate is the best insurance policy.

Real life has more than one ending.

Suddenly I understand what's been staring me in the face. I love you to spite him. I don't love you at all. You don't even fucking exist.

I *want* to love you. I should have loved you with your good looks and your money and your inability to see anyone other than me. You were good for me. You bolstered my high opinion of myself.

But I don't love you! Like God, I enjoyed being adored.

I like being in control. I like winning. Even when it's too late.

I don't love you. I love...*him.*

He's the only one I love!

It's shocking to hear it out loud. I've been plotting my escape so long I've gone blind.

He snaps my diary shut. No need to read any more. Murder isn't an ending, it's a clean slate.

'Go to sleep,' he whispers. 'And when you wake up the world will look different.'

And when I woke up she had disappeared.

The End

'It's not business, it's personal.'
James Lash

I have pieced together the final days of Vivien Lash from her diary, text messages, our conversations about art and love, and the police investigation following her death.

Creepy Neighbour was questioned about the murder of Vivien Lash but he has a rock solid alibi. At the time of her death, he was playing dominoes with UFO in the boiler room, their game captured on the building's security system. UFO won.

The Director was interviewed but he was fighting for his own life the night she disappeared. He loved her. Why would he want to hurt her?

There was a theory that Vivien Lash may have been killed in error. Several witnesses testified that she had been pretending to be somebody else, wearing a wig and big purple gloves, talking Mandarin on her phone.

Elvis was arrested and confessed Vivien Lash's plot to tie up Creepy Neighbour and torture him until he admitted murdering his wife. She must have intended this as a joke.

Elvis protested his innocence but was convicted anyway. It didn't help that he'd worn the Las Vegas jumpsuit at his trial. And explained his theory that my wife had faked her own death so that she could live quietly at Gracelands with the other Elvis.

'All they need is a roll of Sellotape,' he said, looking

hopefully at the judge.

The insurance policy was the nail in his coffin.

'We was Dicks together,' he said, when shown the incriminating document insuring Vivien Lash for a massive amount with the same company who'd already coughed up when his not-so-old mum choked on a cheeseburger.

He broke down when the jury were shown pictures of Vivien Lash's corpse, sobbing into his surprisingly large hands. 'Them pictures look nothing like her.'

The charred corpse soaked in grey water from its holiday in the Thames doesn't look like anyone.

'Elvis is innocent. He don't want the full Joyce Grenfell,' he pleaded as he was led away to start his life sentence.

'It was him!' Elvis shouted, pointing at the public gallery.

But who was he looking at? Creepy Neighbour, slouched into his seat behind me, eyes bleeding into my back. Or the Director, a few rows in front, face serious and pale. I can see why she liked him.

The last words in her diary, written minutes before she died, are:

I want you. Not anyone from the past or future.

Does she mean him or me?

It doesn't matter now.

Shut the book, open it.

No one has kissed me in this room.

Is her diary calculated or spontaneous?

A first draft or something refined and rewritten, like Virginia Woolf's suicide note? Some people prefer the first version.

Writing is prophesy. Don't write anything down unless you want it to come true.

Her ideas are always the best.
I'm almost finished.

There is someone at the door. It's the Director. He doesn't look bad for a man who's been run over by a train.

And no, I didn't push him. My friend fate gave him a helping hand. Distracted by his camera, filming the last shot, fantasising about his escape with her, he didn't see the train until it was too late.

Imagining he had all the time in the world, while the train crept up on him, edging closer; killing his assistant whose head knocked him off the track.

'I need to know what happened to her,' the Director says. Blue shadows beneath his eyes suggest he has not been sleeping. Or maybe his eyes always look that way.

I invite him in. He scans the room, stopping at Stanley Kubrick.

'Is that her?' he asks, leaning in to examine the old picture of my wife and Mr Kubrick standing under a palm tree.

The picture was taken just after she stopped dancing. Her foot had become infected from living in Hyde Park. The bone in her toe will never heal. She says she doesn't mind.

Running his hand over her white marble desk, he asks, 'Is this where she sat?'

Imagining my wife in her stilettos and lip gloss, concentrating on her reflective computer screen, wearing nothing but black pearls and Shanghai silk underwear.

Imagination is all we have in the end.

I gave up my job, our apartment, the life we shared.

Before leaving, I destroyed our possessions. I do not need photographs to remind me of her. I don't need to see her to feel her breath, hear her thoughts, listen to her dreams.

An ending is an opportunity for a beginning. Death is just another kind of resurrection. I need to erase everything and start again.

Sitting in the neon sunset, sipping a martini cocktail (stirred not shaken), she is watching me now. Next time we meet will be the first time.

We're holding hands in the picture I have inside my heart, walking into the future. And our party no longer fears two.

After I had killed her, it was easy.

The End

By the same author:

Lampshades
Dead Glamorous
Penniless in Park Lane

Coming next from Carole Morin:

Liberace's Love Child

'When I was seven, my mother hired me to
murder my father. I'd always wanted to be an
assassin and I had to get the job done by my
eighth birthday...'

www.carolemorin.co.uk

Dragon Ink
London